SQUATTER'S RIGHTS

**Center Point
Large Print**

**This Large Print Book carries the
Seal of Approval of N.A.V.H.**

SQUATTER'S RIGHTS

LAURAN PAINE

CENTER POINT PUBLISHING
THORNDIKE, MAINE

This Center Point Large Print edition
is published in the year 2006 by arrangement with
Golden West Literary Agency.

The text of this Large Print edition is unabridged. In other
aspects, this book may vary from the original edition. Printed in
Thailand. Set in 16-point Times New Roman type.

ISBN 1-58547-697-8

Library of Congress Cataloging-in-Publication Data

Paine, Lauran.
    Squatter's rights / Lauran Paine.--Center Point large print ed.
        p. cm.
    Originally published under pseudonym Will Bradford. London : Robert Hale & Co., c1973.
    ISBN 1-58547-697-8 (lib. bdg. : alk. paper)
        1. Large type books. I. Title.

PS3566.A34S64 2006
813'.54--dc22

                                                                    2005020098

SQUATTER'S RIGHTS

Chapter One

THE LARAMIE PLAINS

"You go south from Laramie with the mountains on your right and a hell of a lot of nothin' on your left, Mister, and you can't miss it because there ain't another town down there until you reach Virginia Dale, and that's over the line into Colorado."

As regional directions went, those wouldn't have been very satisfactory in a great many places, but in Wyoming they were entirely adequate for the elemental reason that they were perfectly correct. Between the town of Laramie, in Wyoming, and the stage-stop and way-station of Virginia Dale, in far northern Colorado, there was just one other clutch of buildings: Jelm, Wyoming.

If there had been any error in the directions the telegrapher gave the Pinkerton detective, it had been in the reference to Jelm as a 'town'. It wouldn't even be a *village* for part of another decade, when the railroad came north from Denver on its way to Laramie and Cheyenne, but the windy, bitterly cold day the burly Pinkerton detective boarded the southbound stage for Jelm, the place had one big general store, one saloon, a stage-station, and a combination fourth-class post office and café.

Those things were on the east side of the road, along with the great holdings of an old grizzled cowman named Grant Maxwell. On beyond the Maxwell range were those mountains, while across the road on the west side—and also north and southward—was more grazing range, most of it as flat as a man's palm. When the wind blew, as it did in all the Laramie Plains country a good bit of the time, spring, winter and autumn, even the Indians who had once owned all that immense grassland gave up trying to keep their lodges upright and went down below the cutbanks to make their villages.

The white man was a superior engineer. When he built he notched logs into place that not even the worst wind could budge. The Maxwell ranch had log buildings, but it was also set in a slight swale, not especially for protection, although nothing put a man's nerves on edge like wind, day in and day out, but because there was a creek there, and some wonderful old cottonwood trees to break the monotony of the flat prairie.

Maxwell's home-ranch was a genuine piece of paradise in the vast emptiness of the cow country around Jelm. It was one of those places that, when a man rode down to it over the plain, and saw the creek, the shade of trees, the huge log barn and house, the clustering outbuildings, it made him feel as though he had just escaped some nameless fate and had reached civilization.

In a way he had. Grant Maxwell, a widower now six

years, up in his fifties, big and weathered and as hard as stone, ruled a bunkhouse of six riders and a range-boss as though he were a feudal baron.

His daughter had married a mining man and had gone out to Nevada the year before her mother died, and his son, Grant Junior, leeched off his father and lived down in Denver—a drunk and a gambler, so it was rumored.

But Maxwell seemed unchanged to those who had known him longest: other cattlemen, like John Frazier, west of Jelm, and Harold Tappan, who ran cattle southeastward, in the plateaux and broken-hills country down around Virginia Dale.

He was the law, at least as far as his range was concerned, and upon the rare occasions when they had to lock up someone in the root-cellar below the saloon in Jelm—the nearest Jelm had to a jail—they usually consulted Grant Maxwell first, if possible, and if that wasn't possible, why then they sent someone out from 'town' to tell him afterwards.

It was said he had been asked to run for senator and had declined. The lawmen up at Laramie, and from southward, down around Denver, had a world of respect for Grant Maxwell.

There were, just naturally, some things he did not particularly approve of, but Maxwell had never been known as a vindictive or blindly biased man. One of those things was what had inclined him to decline to run for senator: equal rights, and the vote, for females. It was not that big Grant Maxwell was

11

unsympathetic to women, he wasn't; he was courtly, in the old-fashioned way, gallant, and had been indulgent to both his wife and daughter. And his aversion to giving women the vote and equal rights was not, as it was with most other men, because he considered them less intelligent than men. It was simply that Wyoming and Colorado were new territories, there was violence somewhere almost every day, and Grant Maxwell, who had been married a long time before his wife died, knew that women could not cope with violence. He had said often enough that probably, someday, the border country between Laramie and Fort Collins, the nearest large town below Virginia Dale, would not need guns and hangropes, *then* he'd favor equal rights for women.

The other thing Grant Maxwell did not favor was the Federal Land Act that gave preference to free land to former soldiers and sailors. But again, it was not because he opposed former soldiers or seamen. It was because he, who had come to the Laramie Plains country as a young man and had bet his life, literally, that he could take and hold his fifty-mile range, knew only too well that no one could make his living off one square mile, a section, or 640 acres, of the kind of land the plains were made of, and when those damned bureaucrats back in Washington parceled out land patents as though they were giving people a corner of paradise, all they were really doing was ruining a lot of very hopeful men, most of them with families, and also they were cluttering up cow country with a lot of sod houses, bean patches, and people whose eventual starvation would drive them to eat beef with Maxwell's—as well as other cowmen's—brands on the hides.

He told a court this, upon the most recent occasion when a desperate homesteader had been caught butchering a three-year-old GM steer. That was in late winter, on a fiercely windy, cold day, when the circuit-riding judge from Cheyenne held court in Ellis Burton's general store in Jelm. And he had stood there, big and gray and scowling, not *asking* the judge for leniency, but *telling* him that to hang a man for trying to feed his family was a far worse crime than cattle rustling, something the judge, whose name was Alexander Curtin, was notorious for hanging men for. Cattle rustling and horse stealing, Judge Curtin had said many times, in public, were the twin evils that most seriously plagued the frontier, and should be stamped out without mercy.

But Judge Curtin's job was a political one and Grant Maxwell, without caring one damned bit that this was so, carried a lot of influence in southern Wyoming, so Alexander Curtin had not sent the squatter to the gallows—he had sent him to prison for ten years. Grant Maxwell went to the man's wife, paid twice what the homestead was worth, sent four of his riders to pack her wagon and see her, with her three children, to the rails-end down in Colorado, on her way back to Ohio, where she had come from. About the ten-year jail sentence he could do little, but he and Alexander Curtin,

13

who had been acquaintances before, did not speak after this interlude.

The trouble, of course, was not that simple. Washington continued to issue grants to land, and homesteaders—full of high spirits and resolve—continued to roll west in their laden wagons. All the wealthy cowmen in Wyoming—and Colorado as well, for that matter—could not have pooled their money and bought out every one that went belly-up. Maxwell wrote stinging letters to everyone from Wyoming's representatives in the Congress and the Senate to the President himself. For all the good that did he might as well gone out and tried to whistle against the wind. The squatters continued to come. The rangemen in other areas took harsher means for getting rid of them, but around Jelm, although there was bitter talk, and a very noticeable hostility when one of those laden wagons rolled up out front of the general store, there was no violence.

In other areas they fired the houses and haystacks of squatters. Around Jelm they couldn't very well burn out people who lived, like prairie dogs, in sod houses that were two-thirds underground, and whose roofs were made of rushes plastered over with mud. There was timber in the mountains, but it was many miles away, and even if most of the sodbusters had owned the big wagons required for hauling whole trees for logs, or had the kinds of teams needed to move such loads, it still would have taken most of a summer to get up there, fell and load enough trees, and get back before snow flew, and what even the dumbest home-steader realized as soon as he found his section on the plains, was that he had to get shelter for his family immediately. That was why the soddies were so common. They were nowhere nearly as good as a log house; the walls seeped melting snow-water all winter long, and the roofs usually dripped too, but at least with an iron stove and a big pile of buffalo chips, or dried cow chips, they could be kept warm. Barring sickness—which struck every winter and usually carried off children first—squatters could usually make it through one winter. The next spring they either were dead of illness, gave up and reloaded their wagons and went back to Ohio or wherever they had come from, or else they pooled their wagons and teams and went to the mountains for logs to build decent residences.

The ones who stayed and built log houses were a very small minority, but the ones who perished or who left, white as slugs from wintering underground, passed fresh families on the march each spring, so, while the faces changed, the problem remained as bad as ever. And it got worse, after a while, for the range cattlemen whose beef losses crept past the degree of tolerance, and *that* was when the squatters had two deadly enemies, nature and the cowmen.

But old Grant Maxwell had established a kind of precedent the time he told Judge Curtin that hanging starving people for trying to fill the stomachs of their kids and womenfolk wasn't the answer, so, at least for a time around Jelm, although the cattlemen and their riders were grim and bitter, there were no lynchings. There *were* a few brawls, but the squatters learned to stay out of Jelm unless they simply had to drive in for supplies, and to avoid the village most of all on Saturday nights when the riders came down to the saloon for poker and serious drinking.

John Frazier told Maxwell one Saturday afternoon out front of the post office that he had lost three cows, not steers, cows that gave him calves every year and were therefore the foundation of his livelihood; that he had found the hides buried in a shallow trench, with his brand on them.

"The damned fools didn't even have sense enough to cut out my mark. And I know which ones did it, Grant, and by gawd I'm not going to stand for this. I know how you feel, and I think you're plumb right, but we can't hang land office clerks who are back in Washington, can we?"

Chapter Two

A BAD NIGHT

A man named Slade, Jake Slade, had once been stationmaster for the stageline down at Virginia Dale. He had survived a wild gunfight—which left one wall of the stage station propped up from out back because it had been so badly riddled with shotgun pellets—and had remained a terror in the countryside until, finally, he had been driven off. Jake Slade died up in Montana in another gunfight, but that came later. After his departure from Virginia Dale everyone breathed easier. He'd led a gang of thoroughly treacherous horse and cattle thieves, and no one ever knew how many murders Slade and his crew had committed, but every now and then a shallow grave would yield up a victim thought to have been robbed and murdered either by Jake himself or some of his killers.

During Slade's heyday Grant Maxwell had hired only gun-handy cowboys. He and Jake had met several times, but Slade, rabid as he was, was not a fool. He had never killed a GM rider and had never stolen either GM horses or cattle.

But that was past now. People were even beginning to make a two-gun Robin Hood out of Slade, which disgusted the men like Grant Maxwell who had known Slade. He told some men at the bar in Jelm one evening in early spring, with the wind howling outside, that there was no way to make a man like Jake Slade look good; that he had been a murderer, a thief, and a liar, all things rangemen did not hold with in anyone. One of Harold Tappan's riders from down around Virginia Dale, who was repping for his employer during a spring turn-out and separation, said, "Mister Maxwell, I've known lawmen who did all those things," and old Grant had shot back his answer to that.

"I just told you—rangemen don't hold with that

kind of a person, no matter *who* he is. I didn't say lawmen were a damned bit better. But I believe most of them are."

The rangerider leaned and pulled on his big, droopy moustache, and thoughtfully drank his whisky, and eventually he said, "Did you fellers hear about the robbery down in Fort Collins?" No one had. "Well, the way we got it down at Virginia Dale, from a stage driver, was that this feller walked into the Drovers and Merchants Bank down there with a tow-sack in one hand and a nickel-plated pistol in the other hand, and made them folks fill his sack. Then he run outside and jumped on his horse, and a feller who'd been in the bank run out and got off two shots, and winged this outlaw."

Someone asked which way the outlaw had fled. The cowboy said, "East, is the way I heard it, riding sloppy in the saddle like a man'd ride who was hurt."

"Any reward?"

The lanky rider didn't know about that. "The driver didn't say. But if there ain't one now, I'll bet there'll be one in a day or two. He made off with eight thousand dollars."

The barman groaned aloud. "Eight thousand dollars. Gawd a'mighty, that's more'n a feller can make in his whole darned lifetime."

The enormity of the fortune drove everyone into a long silence, then a youthful man who rode for John Frazier, and who had not been on the Laramie Plains long, drew upon his memory to make the next comment. "Sounds about like the same feller who made off with an army payroll over in the Yellowstone country. Leastwise that's the same way the outlaw done it over there. Only thing folks remembered was that he held the sack in his right hand and the nickel-plated gun in his left hand. That time he got off with two thousand."

The bartender thought aloud. "If it's the same outlaw, he'd ought to be about ready to retire."

Grant Maxwell hunched up inside his coat and turned to leave. Outlaws were the least of his problems. He had been told that same morning, early, before the crew had ridden out, that someone had butchered a GM steer north of Jelm on one of the Laramie Township sections. He hadn't mentioned it at the bar, for obvious reasons. Now, even if he had mentioned it, that outlaw who had raided the bank down in Fort Collins would have taken precedent.

Outside, the wind was knife-blade sharp. Maxwell tipped up his fur-pelt collar, and turned as a loose-moving, long-faced, lanky cowboy ambled up. It was Jess Farley, Maxwell's rangeboss, and he had a letter in his gloved hand which he handed over wordlessly. Grant's daughter corresponded regularly. Her weekly letter was a high-point in Maxwell's routine. As Maxwell accepted the letter he and the dark-eyed rangeboss exchanged a look. There was no letter from Grant Maxwell's son, down in Denver, which was a lot closer than Nevada. There very rarely was a letter from Grant Junior.

Farley said, "Going to freeze hard tonight," and turned to glance up the bleak little treeless, ugly roadway in the direction of the stage station, where a palisaded pole fence formed a surround for the live-stock kept out back. "Seems to me, if the In'ians'd had any sense, they'd have given the Laramie Plains to us whites, then slipped down to Arizona or California where it's always warm, and laughed themselves to death."

Maxwell smiled. Jess Farley had been saying unkind things about the plains country ever since he'd first gone to work as a twelve-dollar-a-month cowboy for Grant Maxwell, seven years earlier, and he was still in it.

"Go on inside out of the wind and have a drink," he told his rangeboss. "There's a story one of Tappan's men told about a big holdup down in Fort Collins the last day or two."

Farley nodded, watching the craggy profile of his employer. "All right," he said, but did not move out of his tracks. "Did you tell 'em about that steer?"

Maxwell shook his head. "No. What's the point, Jess? They'll get tanked up on firewater soon enough, and go off half-cocked and lynch a squatter one of these nights."

"Well, but it's gettin' to the place where I'd be glad to see the wolves and bears come back."

Maxwell held his daughter's letter in both hands and gravely considered it, with wind howling under the pole eaves above him. "You ever been inside one of those soddies, Jess?"

"Nope. Never had a hankering to go inside one."

Grant pocketed the letter and looked up where a thin, cold moon was hanging. "I have. It reminded me of those In'ians I helped put in the cattle cars down at Fort Collins to be shipped down to Indian Territory for relocation. The people have the same look, and the soddies smell about as bad as those cars smelled. I had my wars with In'ians, Jess, but my gawd, I couldn't look 'em in the eye that day."

"But the In'ians didn't have no claim to the land," said Farley, "and these people got the government behind 'em, so—"

"Jess," drawled the older man, shoving fisted hands deep inside his jacket pockets, "I think the Indians had a sight better claim to it than these sodbusters have; at least the In'ians knew how to survive here. They held it against all comers, until we arrived. But the government took care of the In'ians, and now it's doing the same thing for those squatters, and it's doing the same damned wrong things all over again." Grant faced his rangeboss. "You know what I think, Jess? I think there's no such thing as a real good government; there are just different kinds of conspiracies by politicians that belong to different parties."

Farley was a quiet, completely honest, hard-working rangeman, and that was all he wanted to be. Politics were as alien to him as the moon. More so, perhaps; at least he could *see* the moon, and the only political office-holder he'd ever seen around Jelm was Judge

Curtin. He started past to enter the saloon. "See you in the morning," he said, and entered the building behind Maxwell's back.

It wasn't much of a ride from the village to the head-quarters ranch for Grant Maxwell, and he was dressed for the cold and wind. He was also accustomed to them both. Even the snow no longer troubled him. After spending most of his adult life devising protective means for mitigating Wyoming's bitter extremes in weather, he had inured himself, and he had also done what could be done to protect his livestock. He had planted windbreaks, which were fifty feet tall now, and wind-proof; he had erected additional log barns here and there on his fifty miles of deeded land and kept them filled with wild hay against the four-foot snowfalls.

What he had no protection against was exactly what he and Jess had discussed out front of the saloon, and the reason was simply because, although he had been raided a few times by professional rustlers—and had hanged his share of them—this wasn't really rustling; not the way Alexander Curtin claimed that it was.

As for that steer Jess had found butchered on the range, he could stand some of this. He did not like it and he did not approve of it either, but one steer, even ten steers, wouldn't come anywhere near to bankrupting him, and meanwhile he would give thought to a cure. There had to be one. Hanging every haggard, shrunken-gutted, demoralized and desperate squatter who killed a beef to stay alive sure as hell was no

22

answer. In the first place, there weren't enough ropes. In the second place, violence begot violence. And in the third place— He suddenly saw a low-held lantern swing wildly about a half-mile ahead of him, to the north, out across the range. His horse snorted and stopped spraddle-legged. Maxwell instinctively but unhurriedly unbuttoned the lower segment of his riding coat and pulled the thong off the hammer of his holstered Colt.

He was at a loss as to who would be out there in the moonless night in weather like this. Then it dawned on him. A squatter! A damned steer-killing squatter! And this one was a complete fool because, even if he hadn't had that lantern along, he was working on a downed animal less than a mile from Jelm and about two miles from the headquarters of GM, in an area Maxwell's riders had made a deep trail coming and going.

He urged the horse ahead, but it went only very reluctantly, which probably meant that it had smelled blood. Maxwell shed his right-hand glove, drew his six-gun and hooked the horse to force it onward. He got almost within sight of the man before a horse nickered out there. Someone instantly doused the lantern. But it was much too late for that. Grant Maxwell hooked the horse hard, again, and when it loped a big gust of wind coming from the east carried the sound of a man swearing in an unsteady voice, as though he were having trouble mounting.

Maxwell saw the critter half-skinned, and his horse

shied violently around it. He fought the horse a moment. Out in the stormy night a horse sped away on steel shoes and Grant Maxwell tried one sound-shot, then another one, and although he gave chase, the squatter got away.

Maxwell turned back and got stiffly down to be sure the dead steer's throat had been cut, then he remounted and headed for the ranch to find someone to send back with a wagon for the beef.

He was angry all the way through; about half as much because this beef-killing homesteader had been insolent enough to try and butcher a GM critter practically in his ranch yard, as because the man had killed the steer.

He reached the log barn and tied his horse, stamped over to the bunkhouse and interrupted a poker session to send two big-eyed riders back with the wagon. Then, without giving more than the skimpiest details, he went back to the barn to care for his horse—and found blood on the animal's fetlocks. He ran a hand down, feeling for a wound, but there was none, so, assuming it was blood from the butchered steer, he off-saddled and turned the horse out, then, as he was walking back up through the barn, it occurred to him that *this* blood was too fresh to have come from the dead steer.

He stopped just beyond the barn opening to watch his two riders, bundled against the cold, harnessing a team to a wagon. If that blood hadn't come from the steer, which had been dead probably an hour by the time Maxwell got to it, then it had come from—the squatter? He had fired twice, and neither time did he have a real target. But sometimes a sound-shot was accurate, not often, but sometimes.

The wind was increasing, and now it had little stinging particles of either driven snow or sleet in it. It was a bad night for a man to be lying out there bleeding from a forty-five slug.

Even a damned beef-stealing squatter deserved better than that. He considered taking another man or two with him, then decided this was his doings, his riders shouldn't have to go out tonight after having already put in a long day.

He turned back into the barn to catch and saddle a fresh horse.

Chapter Three

SQUATTERS

Maxwell rode out with the two men on the wagon and they may have thought he did this to guide them. It was too bitter and stormy for any conversation, and he wasn't in the mood for it anyway, but when they reached the carcass and he got down to help load it, one of the riders jerked up the head and showed his partner and his employer the little hole in the whorl of hair between and slightly above the eyes, and

Maxwell said, "I saw him. Well, I didn't really *see* him, but I glimpsed a gray horse and I *heard* him running for it."

The riders waited after the beef was loaded, but Maxwell gestured them back to the ranch, and although they watched with interest as he led his horse around, quartering for sign in the darkness, neither of them spoke until they were heading home, then one leaned and said, over the howling wind, "If he figures to find tracks on a night like this, he's sure goin' to be disappointed."

But Grant Maxwell was not interested in tracks, although he did find where a horse had been standing, and where boot-tracks came running, stamping down the moist earth. What he sought, and eventually found, was red blood on the four-inch-high wiry springtime grass, and it was a good fifty yards from where the steer had been shot, so it had come from either the squatter or his horse.

Maxwell went along, bent half over, leading his mount, following the steel-shod tracks about a hundred yards and was satisfied that the horse had not been hard hit. He was moving too freely and there was no more blood until, near where Maxwell stopped trying to read sign, he found a streak of it where the wind was whipping the grass against his chaps. He felt it. It was cold, of course, but it was not dried yet, even though it was cold and getting colder.

He got back across leather and sat a moment rummaging in his mind for the location of the nearest soddies. There were no homesteaders on his deeded land, but northward and across the stageroad eastward, where John Frazier ran cattle on public domain—called 'freegraze'—there were three homesteads within a three-mile radius. Unless the man he had shot was a complete stranger, wounded as he was, without much doubt he would seek help, and, being a squatter, he would know where the nearest soddies were.

Maxwell raised his face to test the weather. It was too late in the spring for a real norther, so even if that was snow being blown along, it wouldn't stick. As for the wind, well, this was the windy time of year on the Laramie Plains. *Any*time was the windy time, but more so in the early spring.

He turned back towards Jelm unmindful of the time, but it wasn't very late. The storm had darkened the world prematurely.

When he reached the village and tied up out front of the saloon to shed his gloves before entering, two men came forth with orange lamplight behind them. One was Jess Farley, the other was another older man, a rider named Buck Alden. They both squinted in surprise, then Jess walked on over where Grant Maxwell was standing beside his horse.

"Thought you went back," he said.

"Rode up on to someone butchering a steer no more'n a mile from town, got off a couple of shots and winged him, I think." Maxwell looked up. "You can go on home, Buck."

Alden, who hadn't been able to hear the conversation, nodded and went to his horse. Jess Farley reached for his gloves and thoughtfully drew them on. Then, as he raised his thin face he said, "Maybe we might need him."

Maxwell, reaching for his reins, shook his head. He said nothing until they were riding northward into the teeth of the icy wind, and because of this he had to lean and shout to make himself heard. He gave Jess the facts as he knew them, and pointed off to the west in the direction of the nearest soddy. "We'll try them all. While I'm talking, you look for a gray horse with saddle-sweat on him. And blood."

Jess pulled his hat so low he had to peer from under the brim. He also rolled up the collar of his rider's coat and hunched his wide, bony shoulders against the force of the storm. He said, "What a lousy damned night to go after meat," but because the wind whipped the words away Grant Maxwell did not hear them.

The first soddy had been built by a man named Hovic, but he hadn't even lasted out the first winter, and now some new squatters were living in it. They came and went; generally, the cattlemen and their riders kept entirely aloof from homesteaders. When Maxwell and Farley were close enough to make out the four-foot walls above the surface of the ground, and the mud-wattle roof, Maxwell caught the smell of a buffalo-chip fire. He reached to loosen the lower half of his coat and to slip off the tie-down where it kept his six-gun from being shaken out of his holster while he was a-horseback. The reason was because squatters hoarded coal-oil for their lamps as much as they hoarded their fuel supply, dried buffalo and cow dung, and normally they retired when the sun went down, but evidently these people didn't.

There was no light showing, but then there was no way for it to show until someone opened a door, because soddies did not have windows.

Grant Maxwell dismounted and stamped his feet to get the stiffness out of his legs. He motioned for Jess to ride around the house, where there was a sod lean-to for whatever livestock the homesteader owned.

There were two kinds of soddy doors, one was slanted at ground level and a person went down a log ladder just below; the other kind was a regular door with the earth dug out on both sides to make an incline down to it. This soddy had the latter kind of an entrance. Grant Maxwell, tugging off his gloves and pocketing them, went down the slight incline, and here, for the first time since leaving his own barn, the wind could not reach him.

He balled up a big fist and rattled the door with it. Then he put the same big hand around the butt of his six-gun while he waited.

A frightened, thin voice called from within. "Who is it? Go on over to the town; it's only a mile from here."

It was closer to two miles to Jelm. Maxwell said, "It's Grant Maxwell. I want to talk to you folks. Open up."

For ten seconds there was no more sound and Grant was considering his next move when the door opened

29

a crack and someone beyond Maxwell's sight shoved a long-barreled Springfield rifle barrel through. He knocked the thing aside. The door swung wide and a thin, graying woman wrapped in a soiled old brown blanket looked up at him out of a face twisted and made ugly with terror.

He stepped inside, took the rifle from the woman and leaned it aside. The soddy was warm and a stub of a candle was burning. The place smelled of greasy cooking and human sweat. Maxwell looked over where three bunks had been built one above the other against the far wall. A boy of about ten or twelve years was staring out of enormous dark eyes from the top bunk. The lower one was empty, with an old moth-eaten buffalo robe trailing to the damp floor where the woman had evidently been sleeping. The middle bunk was empty and did not look as though it had been slept in for some time.

Otherwise, there was a table where the candle was, and three wooden boxes arranged one atop the other, as a cupboard. A blanket partitioned off one corner of the soddy.

The woman stood clutching the blanket to her skinny body. Grant Maxwell was a big man, but in his lined coat, with his black hat pulled low, and with his weathered, unsmiling face, he looked a foot taller, a foot wider, and bleakly murderous. He knew it; he saw it in their faces. He reached up and shoved back the hat, then he loosened his coat as he said, "Ma'm, where's your mister?" He tried to make it as soft as he could, but neither the woman nor the half-grown boy loosened towards him.

"Not here," said the woman, scarcely audible, although it was still as death in the soddy.

"All right, ma'm, I reckon he isn't. But where is he?"

"Him and some others went to the forest for logs two days back—Mister Maxwell. They'll be back maybe in another two days."

"Who else stays with you folks?"

The woman's fear was leaving a little at a time because of this questioning. "Who stays with us? There's only the three of us. Me, my husband, and our boy. He's yonder in the top bed."

Grant looked over. He smiled. The boy did not move, did not even seem to be breathing. The door opened and Jess Farley ducked to get under the baulk. He was as tall as his employer but not as thick. But Jess was dark, and in the weak, guttery light of the candle he looked anything but reassuring. He had reason not to look pleasant. Without a word he held out a soggy red cloth. Grant Maxwell took it from Jess's gloved hand, and felt the coldness of the wet blood upon his fingers.

Farley said, "Found it out in the lean-to under some meadow-hay in a wooden tub they use for a manger." He looked at the woman, at the boy, then studied the room, and without another word strode over and yanked back the blanket that curtained off a corner of the room. There was no one back there; evidently this

31

was where the older people dressed. Jess turned and went back across by the door.

Maxwell held the bloody rag out to the woman. She leaned, chicken-like, and stared. "You found that in our barn?" she murmured, without looking up at Jess Farley. He did not answer and she reached out with a thin hand to feel the cloth. "Why, that's fresh blood," she said, and recoiled in surprise.

Maxwell, who had been watching her, turned to his rangeboss. "Any stock out there?"

"None," replied Farley.

Maxwell turned back to the woman. "Ma'm, who among your neighbors owns a gray horse?"

The woman thought, then said, "I believe the new folks who settled in two miles northeast have a gray horse. They got a fine team of big sorrels, I know, for me'n my boy was out looking for berries along the creek and saw a pair of big sorrel horses grazing along, out there. I don't know their names—those folks, I mean—they just settled in about two months ago, and we've had sickness so didn't walk over to pay a call like folks should. I think I saw the man riding a gray horse."

Maxwell shoved the bloody rag into his pocket, pulled down his hat, and tugged on his gloves. Then he said, "I'm sorry to have scairt you folks, bustin' in so late and all. Thank you, ma'm."

From beyond the yellow candlelight the boy said, "Mister Maxwell, did you shoot someone?"

The woman turned like a wasp. "Jamie, for heaven's

sake, what an awful thing to say." He turned back, fearful again. "You got to excuse him, Mister Maxwell, he's just upset or he wouldn't bust out with something like that."

Maxwell looked over across the room. "No, I didn't shoot anyone." He smiled. "Sorry I got you up."

Jess held the door and walked out after his employer. Up where the horses were, there were sharp, icy stars showing and the wind was dying. It was no longer spitting sleet either, as they got astride and headed northeast.

Jess said, "He's hit all right. He probably had to duck into the lean-to to re-tie his bandage. If he's hit hard, I'll say one thing for him—he's tough."

They rode on a diagonal course. Both of them knew where the soddy was they were heading for, but neither of them had ever known any of the people who had lived in it, neither those who had built it and who had left as soon as the ground was hard enough to hold up their wagon in the springtime, nor the others who had also come, wraith-like, to spend one winter, then also depart.

Until the scrawny woman had said there was another family living in the soddy on ahead, Maxwell had thought it had been completely abandoned. He very rarely had occasion to ride among the soddies, and excepting this particular night, had felt no inclination to ride among them in a very long while.

Jess pointed to the dark-hulking outline up ahead. They were close enough to smell smoke, but this time

33

it was made by a wood fire. Out back, visible over the low roof, was a pole corral. It hadn't been built very long because the peeled logs were still pale enough to reflect what little light there was in the gusty night.

"More ambitious than most," said Grant, and his rangeboss answered while loosening his coat and touching the free-moving butt of his six-gun.

"Ought to be, if they're eating well."

A horse nickered and a pair of sixteen-hundred-pound draft animals, sorrels with light manes and tails, came ambling out of the northward gloom.

Maxwell and Farley halted. Those animals were the kind people owned who appreciated good horseflesh. They were worth a lot of money. Jess looked on ahead at the soddy and said, "This time maybe I'd better back you up at the door."

Chapter Four

MAXWELL'S 'FEELING'

There was no one around. They opened the door and looked in. There was a cast-iron stove, still with glowing embers, and the soddy was pleasantly warm. There were two lamps hanging from above and both were warm to Maxwell's touch. The place smelled of tobacco smoke and a recent meal. It was a better soddy by far than the first one he and Jess had visited.

This one even had plank walls, and of course the wood would warp and rot eventually, but right now, in the gloom, the interior looked like the interior of a regular house.

Jess mentioned searching the place, but Grant Maxwell refused. They went out back, trailing their horses after them. The big sorrels followed as solemn as a pair of undertakers.

There was a lean-to, an old sod one, and beyond it, roofed-over and two-thirds completed, was a larger, roomier, pole shed, but excepting the big sorrels there was not a sign of life anywhere.

Farley was uneasy and showed it the way he kept looking over his shoulder, scanning the night, and keeping a careful eye cocked towards the soddy from time to time. Eventually he said, "It'd be bad enough, around here, without that damned wind moaning," and his employer agreed.

"Yeah. Look in the sod lean-to, Jess, and I'll look in the other one."

They found nothing, but Grant Maxwell noticed that two horses had recently been inside the partially-completed shed. He found a small hay-ball that was still wet, and examined it in his gloved hands before walking back where the rangeboss was. Jess shook his head without commenting.

Maxwell handed over the hay-ball and Jess studied it, then tossed it down. "They got a horse whose teeth need floating," he deduced, and Maxwell said, "It's fresh. That's the point. That horse that spit it out was here not very long ago. Well, let's go back." Maxwell went over and mounted. As Farley did the same a wolf howled somewhere to the west, and he could not have been very distant or the wind would have masked the sound.

Grant Maxwell was fairly certain of one thing: wherever the squatters had gone, they had *not* gone west or that wolf wouldn't be over there. He debated with himself about making a horseback search, but decided against it when the wind brisked up again. He turned and headed for Jelm, and beyond that, for the ranch. By the time he and Jess Farley reached the log barn the wind was beginning to abate again.

As they were dismounting, Jess said, "It puzzles me. Where did they all go?"

Maxwell had a feeling about that. "To take care of the wounded man."

Farley went to light the lantern upon the near wall as he replied to that. "Sure, but *where?* On a clear night you can see a mile in all directions, and if that feller's hit as hard as I figure he's got to be, where could they take him that he'd be out of the weather? It'd have to be somewhere they got a light."

Grant Maxwell removed his saddle and blanket and went to pitch them across the saddle-pole, then he returned to slip off the bridle and take the horse out to a corral. Jess had a point; if the wounded man's friends were looking after him they'd need a warm, dry, lighted place. Of course there was that other soddy, the third one, the soddy they hadn't ridden on out to search for and visit. That was a possibility.

Jess made a cigarette, standing by the lantern with its silvery reflector throwing out whiteness around his hat-shadowed face. He was waiting for Grant Maxwell to say something. Grant did. He said, "Thanks for coming along; now you'd better get some sleep."

Farley accepted that with stoic equanimity. "And tomorrow?"

Grant, who rarely smoked and never cigarettes, only a pipe, came over to stand in the white light too. He was thoughtful. "The steer keeps looking less and less important," he mused. "Jess, the soddy's got wood walls, there was plenty of real firewood, good tables and beds, that team—I don't think we have one as good—and the other things . . ." Grant shook his head at his rangeboss. "They are too prosperous to risk getting lynched butchering a steer, and it makes even less sense when you figure how one of them tried that—practically athwart the trail we use going to town and returning."

Jess smoked, leaned upon the log wall, and grew pensive. "Well, maybe they ain't always been so prosperous; maybe they been eating stolen beef so long that even now when they're prosperous, they hate to pay good money for it."

Maxwell said, "Yeah, maybe," and headed for the front opening. "See you in the morning. Mind that lantern."

Jess turned to 'mind' the lantern, and afterwards

went along to the darkened bunkhouse. Inside, although there had inevitably been a little flurry of excitement, no one was still awake to question the foreman when he walked in.

At the big house where Grant Maxwell now lived alone, rattling around in all those rooms like a small stone in a big barrel, there was a damp chilliness. He had to build a roaring fire in the black old stone fire-place just to get the dampness to depart, and while he waited, still in his coat and hat, he got himself a stiff one from the dining-room sideboard and took the glass back into the parlor with him, where he sat all loose and relaxed, upon the horsehair-stuffed big old leather sofa, staring into the fire.

He was not sleepy. That would come later, when the house got warm, when his chilled body began to let down a little after being wind-buffeted and tense for so long.

Some men had exceptionally developed instincts. Grant Maxwell was such a man. He had, during the course of his earlier years, been able to 'feel' danger, when other men felt nothing and blundered head-first into trouble. He had a feeling, now, that winging that squatter was not going to end simply, and by the time the house was warm and the whisky had made him drowsy, he had almost forgotten the butchered steer.

He went to bed tired, and the following morning he awakened to a perfect day. The wind was gone, the sun was coming early, the yard was peaceful, and a thin little spindrift of smoke was already rising from the bunkhouse tin smokestack. Someone was down forking feed to the corralled saddle stock. He could hear the squealing as the feed was thrown over the fence and the horses rushed towards it.

There was even birdsong in the treetops, which was unusual, except that this was springtime and birds, like all other animate things, were busy at the blind urge that made so much turmoil among living things this time of year.

Grant rose and took his time getting ready for breakfast. The ranch cook was an old man, older even than his employer, and he was also slightly lame, with a 'misery' in his back, and no one, not even Grant Maxwell himself, ever appeared in his huge kitchen until he rang the ship's bell that was just outside the back porch, atop a ten-foot cedar post.

The cook had been with Maxwell seven years. He was a reformed drunk from Cheyenne and could quote from the Bible at the drop of a hat. As Jess Farley had once commented, "Old Gimpy's one of those fellers who goes from one extreme to the other. He either wants to daddy you or he hates the sight of you. He either drinks himself to the floor, or he can't even abide smellin' likker on a man's shirt. The world's either hell or heaven, but I'll be damned if he don't know more ways to make bull meat taste like partridge than any woman who ever lived."

There was something else old Gimpy could do. He could whip up a batch of baking-powder biscuits that were so light and delicious the men actually complimented him about that, and compliments from rangeriders, especially towards cooks, were rarer than Second Comings.

The bell rang just as Grant Maxwell was leaving the house by the door in the rear wall of his huge bedroom. He turned back automatically. He'd had in mind having a conference about the day's riding, down at the bunkhouse. Now he'd have it in the kitchen.

Just before closing the door he shot a look towards the well-house; it was beyond this, inside a roofed-over three-quarter shed, that the ranch butchering was done. That steer would be hanging down there waiting to be carved up.

He turned back, and sighted movement far out where the sun was shining. It was a solitary horseman riding in at a walk, and what held Maxwell motionless for a while was the fact that this man was not dressed like a cowboy. Even his hat was different, it had a narrow brim. Until the horseman got closer Maxwell could not make out much more, but instead of heading for the kitchen, he stepped out upon the porch—it ran the full length of the house—and stood watching. The 'feeling' he had was not just of a stranger, but of some *particular* stranger.

Old Gimpy gave the bell one impatient ring, which was meant to serve notice on Maxwell that he would not wait any longer to start serving, and the horseman raised his head at the sound. That was when Maxwell saw that the man was wearing a tie. About the only people addicted to ties on the range were preachers, judges, undertakers and politicians, and, except preachers, none of these types appeared very often. Grant Maxwell was interested, so he left the porch and strolled towards the long tie-rack out front of the barn, which was where the stranger would probably get down and tie up.

Around him, the fragrance of springtime was growing stronger as new-day sunlight and heat increased. This was the best time of year on the Laramie Plains. It lasted about two months, then the heat came, and after that, because two-legged as well as four-legged animals in Wyoming were more accustomed to cold than to heat, summer passed, and no one was sorry to see it go. It was easier to stay warm than it was to get cool.

The barn cast a great shadow, pale but still a shadow, and Grant could hear his horses eating in the corrals out back. A lot of little things gave a man the kind of feeling he had, as he leaned, hat tipped down to shade his eyes, and watched the oncoming stranger. A man's belief in himself, his sense of confidence and conviction arose from those little things, like the sound of horses eating. *His* horses, *his* cattle, *his land* as far, and a lot farther, than he could see.

The stranger veered slightly towards the barn, which meant that he had seen Maxwell leaning there, obviously waiting. When he was close enough the man raised a hand and Grant returned that age-old salute— the sign that a stranger came in peace.

The stranger's mount wasn't much; probably a livery animal, with a plodding walk and dull eyes, but when the man drew rein and said, "Good morning," the horse became insignificant because the stranger was a large, muscular man, probably in his late twenties or early thirties, and he had the look of an individual who would smile or snarl, be a friend or an enemy, upon the turn of a word. As he dismounted Grant returned the greeting, and leaned there waiting.

The stranger moved with heavy, strong self-assurance. When he turned to face Maxwell he tipped back his hat and shoved out a big paw to shake. "You'll be Grant Maxwell?" he asked, and looked pleased when Maxwell confirmed this. As he withdrew his hand and turned to slowly gaze around, he said, "I wouldn't have believed there could be such a place on these damned plains, Mister Maxwell." He laughed quietly, and settled against the tie-rack as though he had nothing more pressing than to be comfortable. "I'm Norman Verrill." He brought forth a small folder and held it open. "Pinkerton detective, Mister Maxwell." He returned the folder to his inside coat pocket. "They told me up in Laramie how to find Jelm, but I reckon it was my fault, but I plumb forgot to ask if Jelm had a liverybarn. It don't have." Norman Verrill's hard, smiling blue eyes went to the horse beside him. "I had to borrow this critter from the storekeeper. You'd know him, I expect."

Maxwell knew him. "Ellis Burton."

Verrill kept smiling. "That's him. He wasn't real anxious to loan me the horse, until I told him I was on my way to see you." The hard, smiling blue eyes looked with frank interest at Grant Maxwell. "You got a name that opens doors around here. At least it opens *barn* doors, Mister Maxwell."

Almost half a century of reading men enabled a person to develop an indefinable ability; Grant Maxwell decided that he did not like this big, powerful young Pinkerton detective, but if he'd had to define his reasons in words, he couldn't have done it.

He said, "Have you had breakfast, Mister Verrill?" and the detective shook his head, still smiling. "Then come along; my men are probably about finished by now, but there'll be plenty left."

Verrill accepted, and without even looking back at the patiently tied horse, crossed the yard, and that, finally, gave Grant Maxwell something concrete to dislike about Norman Verrill; no man, cityman or rangeman, ever went to fill out the wrinkles in his own gut before he saw to it that his horse was cared for, and fed, first.

Chapter Five

GRANT MAXWELL'S VISITOR

The men were trooping out as Maxwell and the big young stranger appeared at the kitchen's rear entrance. Five sets of eyes jumped up in surprise and frankly appraised the stranger. Only one man, Jess Farley, did not show as much interest, but Jess was a naturally discreet man. He nodded as the stranger went past, then he said, speaking to his employer, that maybe the crew ought to look around over among the soddies today, just to make certain there was no more GM beef over there.

Maxwell said, "No. Stay away from over there, Jess. We'll figure out something in time. Today, you boys look to the drift, and whatever you find near the road push back eastward farther on to our range. I'll look you up later, if I get the chance."

Inside, old Gimpy was clearing the big table and making a special point of ignoring the stranger. When Grant Maxwell entered, Gimpy looked up. Like all old men, Gimpy knew when to show temper and when not to. This was one of those times when a man shouldn't do it, so, instead of protesting about having to serve another breakfast, he went bitterly and lamely to fill two more plates and fetch the coffeepot.

Norman Verrill sat down, put his hat aside, and gazed out the window where the six rangeriders were ambling towards the barn. "You've got quite an outfit here," he said, admiration in his voice. "This is the kind that keeps the country strong, Mister Maxwell." The hard, blue eyes dropped back to Maxwell, as Grant sat down across from Verrill. "In my business we deal a lot with folks who don't mind the law, and after a while a man gets so that he starts thinking there's more of the wrong kind of folks than there are the other kind."

Gimpy brought their breakfast and set the coffeepot close with unnecessary roughness; he had to register his disapproval *some* way. Grant lifted his face, they exchanged a look, and old Gimpy wilted as he hitched back towards his washpan and pile of dishes.

Grant Maxwell was a patient man, but not *too* patient. He said, "What brings you out here, Mister Verrill?"

The smiling, humorless blue eyes grew still. Verrill reached for his coffee cup as he answered. "Some banks over in Idaho got robbed a couple of months back, Mister Maxwell. Then one got robbed over in the Yellowstone country not very long ago, and a clerk was killed. And yesterday while I was in Laramie I got a telegram from the San Francisco office that a bank down at Fort Collins got held up." Verrill tasted his coffee. Old Gimpy made excellent coffee. Verrill drank deeply before setting the cup down. "All these banks been robbed by a single outlaw, and he operated

45

the same way. The details in the telegram about the Fort Collins holdup match exactly with the holdups in Idaho and in Wyoming."

Maxwell suddenly remembered something one of his cowboys had said. "Left-handed robber, Mister Verrill?"

The Pinkerton detective, in the act of lifting a forkful of food to his mouth, stopped moving. "If that was a guess it was a plumb good one," he murmured, and now he was no longer smiling. Just the merciless hardness showed.

"No guess," replied Grant Maxwell, and over the big man's shoulder he saw old Gimpy listening for all he was worth. "No guess; one of my riders is from the Yellowstone country. He was telling us last night at the saloon in Jelm about an outlaw who robbed a bank over there. I remember him saying the man was left-handed. At least, he said the outlaw kept his gun in his left hand."

Verrill resumed his feeding, and for a while he was quiet. Then he smiled again. "We take fellers like this and draw lines on a map, Mister Maxwell, and almost every time we get a kind of pattern. Now, this outlaw come east into Wyoming from Idaho—if it's the same man, and I'm confident it is—then he dropped over to Yellowstone, made his strike, then he angled southward down into Colorado, to Fort Collins, but if you studied the lines on my map, you'd see that he went a long way out of his way, for a man traveling easterly, to reach Fort Collins."

Grant Maxwell saw the fallacy in this at once. "Who said he wasn't planning on going southward? He didn't have to keep on traveling eastward, did he?"

Verrill's smile showed appreciation. "No, no one said he had to keep going eastward, for a fact. *But*— an outlaw who specializes in raiding banks, Mister Maxwell, don't usually go southward to hit one lousy bank, like they got in Fort Collins, when by continuing on eastward he could raid a bank in Laramie and, maybe the same day, raid another one in Cheyenne, which is close to Laramie. But that's only part of what the lines on the map show. This feller went *south,* 'way out and around the plains country, and after the Fort Collins raid he disappeared."

"He was wounded down there," said Grant. "One of the cowboys from Virginia Dale heard that from a coach-driver and told us, last night in the saloon at Jelm. A wounded man tries to get help. Even if he's a bankrobber. . . ." Something hit Grant Maxwell, hard, and made him falter. Maybe he *hadn't* winged that squatter last night; maybe the man had already been wounded!

Norman Verrill was watching Maxwell closely. He said, "Something else they talked about in the saloon last night, Mister Maxwell?"

Grant recovered quickly. "Something about a nickel-plated pistol."

Verrill nodded slowly. "That's right. A nickel-plated double-action pistol." Verrill ate again for a moment before resuming their discussion. "What I got to wondering on the stage ride down to Jelm from Laramie, Mister Maxwell, was why this feller, who followed a pattern in his raids until after Yellowstone, suddenly went southward, which broke the pattern."

Maxwell could guess Verrill's thought about this, but he kept this to himself.

"I'll tell you how I figure it, Mister Maxwell: every man's got a place where he lets down. Even an outlaw needs to set down and rest for a spell, don't he? Well, my guess is that this particular outlaw is from out here on the Laramie Plains somewhere, and that's the reason he made that big sashay around this country—because he didn't want anyone to figure, if he hit the banks in Laramie and Cheyenne, he might head south afterwards. You see, a feller who raided as far south as Fort Collins, then rode eastward from there, put all this plains country behind him, and *that* sure makes it look like he didn't know this country, wouldn't you say?"

Grant Maxwell was thinking of something else. He heard everything the detective said, but he was reflecting upon the swift and sudden disappearance of those people from the second soddy last night. Usually, unless people were accustomed to moving that fast, and even then if they had women and youngsters, like the ones he and Jess had encountered at the first soddy, they left someone behind when they fled—if that's what those people had done, who had taken care of the injured man.

Verrill finished his breakfast and mopped up the

gravy with a chunk of wheat bread, then he had a second cup of coffee. He was the size of a man who, if he'd really been hungry, probably could have cleaned up all the Maxwell riders had left.

Then he dug out a tobacco sack and made a smoke, which he lit, and as he blew smoke he said, "There are times when I wish I'd just stayed with working the range. This riding stages day in and day out and never knowing when a man's going to eat next, or bed down, is hard work." He smiled. "To get back; it seemed to me you'd know anyone in the countryside, Mister Maxwell, who might have been absent from home, or maybe might have come back within the last day or so, looking poorly—like maybe he was sick from a gunshot."

Grant Maxwell shook his head. "I don't go visiting much, and running GM takes up all my time. Then there are the squatters, the drifters, the other people who pass through. If it was something to do with my land, or my cattle or horses or riders, I'd know. About all I can tell you is that none of my riders have been absent."

"How about the folks over at Jelm?"

Maxwell shook his head over that too. "I ride in maybe once a week, Saturday night, and have a drink or two. Except for Ellis Burton who owns the general store, and one or two others, like the postmaster and the way-station agent, I only know the folks to nod to."

"There are other cow outfits around?" asked Verrill.

"John Frazier, west of the road. His headquarters are about four miles due west of Jelm. You can't see them from the plain because they are down under a cutbank. But if you'll look for ruts and follow them, they'll take you down there. And there is Harold Tappan, southward at Virginia Dale, which is the next way-station southward after you leave Jelm. It was one of his men who was up here repping for Tappan who told us about the Fort Collins robbery in the saloon last night. Otherwise, you've got to ride a couple of days to find other outfits."

"How about homesteaders?" asked Verrill, drinking from his refilled coffee-cup.

Maxwell told the truth. "I have very little to do with them. Don't know them except by their clothes when I see them, and because there's the usual bad feeling I keep my men on the east side of the road, on our own range. Those people come and go, and it's a damned shame what the government is doing to them."

This last remark elicited raised eyebrows. Norman Verrill, the former rangerider, said, "The government? What's the government doing to them?"

"Sending them out here thinking they can make a living off a section of rangeland that's got hardpan six inches down and gravelly soil above that," exclaimed Grant Maxwell, getting noticeably indignant as he always did when this subject came up.

"This here outlaw could be among those people," said Verrill. It was clear, at once, that Verrill hoped this was the case. Evidently he was a die-hard rangeman. Many lawmen were, even private lawmen like Pinkerton detectives.

Gimpy came to yank away their plates and hobble back to his tub to wash them. That was the signal that breakfast was over. Maxwell rose, and so did the big, younger man. They left the kitchen and strolled out into the warm, sunlighted yard heading for the tie-rack out front of the barn. Except for some chickens that were old Gimpy's private possessions, the yard was empty and quiet. A small band of loose saddle stock grazed out a quarter of a mile, and because the air was so clear and clean they looked much closer.

Verrill stopped and leaned on the tie-rack. He looked thoughtful. "There's one thing you might do to help," he exclaimed. "This here outlaw stole a horse over by the Yellowstone river from a cow camp. It's got a heart branded on the left front shoulder. You could tell anyone you happen to talk to that if they see such a horse they'd ought to send a letter or a telegram to the Pinkerton office down in San Francisco."

Maxwell said, "What color horse?"

Verrill reached to untie his borrowed mount as he answered. "Gray. Pretty fair-using horse, so the cowboys said who had him stolen out of their cavvy, Mister Maxwell." Verrill turned back and offered his hand again, along with his easy smile. "That sure was a fine breakfast. I'm right obliged to you." He turned and stepped up over leather. "I'll probably be by again—unless I get called away when our boy takes to the trail again. But between you an' me, I figure he's

51

holed up around the Laramie Plains country somewhere. Good day, Mister Maxwell, and thanks again."

For five minutes Grant Maxwell leaned on the tie-
rack trying to explain to himself why he had not told
Verrill about the rustler riding the gray horse last
night, who was wounded, and who looked more and
more like the outlaw Verrill was tracking.

He could not come up with a rational reason at all,
excepting one: he did not like Norman Verrill. But that
was hardly an excuse; he had known a lot of lawmen
he had not liked. They'd had that same predatory look,
that same wolf-like killer disposition, and he had co-
operated with them.

Old Gimpy came forth from the back of the big
house with his flour-sack apron held aloft, calling his
chickens, and as stupid as chickens undeniably were,
these had at least learned that when the game-legged
old man came out and called in his scratchy voice, he
was bringing them bits of bread or toast, or whatever
he had salvaged from the breakfast meal, and they ran
squawking from all directions.

Grant Maxwell turned and sauntered on through the
barn heading for the corral, where he meant to catch a
horse. It was in his mind to ride out, find Jess, and
relay to him what the stranger had wanted, who he
was, and what Maxwell himself now thought about
that squatter they had tried to find during the storm
last night.

Chapter Six

AN ALMOST KILLING

Like most range grasses, the graze on the Laramie Plains never got tall, scarcely more than four to six inches in a good, damp-warm spring, but it had amazing strength to it. Two weeks after the cattle had grazed over it their hair began slipping, their new coat came in dark red and shiny, and the wet cows made milk until it dripped.

Grant Maxwell had probably seen as many cattle as any commercial grower his age, and yet each spring-time when he rode the range, it was like it had been the first time. Whatever it was that lay deep down inside a man, and which responded to new calves, sleek cows, and rich grass, was strongly embedded in his soul.

Except that this morning as he loped northeastward looking for his riders, he noticed it a little less.

He could not understand what had made him hold back with Norman Verrill. It troubled him simply because all his life he had been a forthright man, a believer in black and white, right and wrong, yet this morning he had not offered his thoughts, and while of course there was no law that said a man *had* to offer such things, still and all if that damned steer-killing squatter *was* Verrill's outlaw, Grant Maxwell could have, by offering a few perfunctory sentences, settled it one way or another.

Except for one thing: he knew how range justice worked. He also knew that Pinkerton detectives, like all other rangeriding lawmen, did not bring in as many outlaws and suspected outlaws as they ran to earth.

Still, that wasn't his real excuse and he was honest enough with himself to know it wasn't.

Finally, he saw two riders, with a third one far ahead, chousing some wet cows and calves towards the east, and angled to meet them where they came to a line of trees Maxwell had planted for a windbreak near the working grounds, something like thirty years earlier.

The two riders did not see him, or, if they did, since they already had their hands full trying to drive anxious mother-cows and their completely unpredictable little calves, they chose to concentrate on their work and not on another horseman.

But the foremost rider saw him, halted, then turned back and met Maxwell in tree-shade. It was Jess Farley, and he dragged out a blue bandana to mop his face as his employer walked on up and halted. "Sure not used to this weather," said Jess, dark eyes puckered nearly closed even though they were in shade.

Maxwell told his rangeboss who Norman Verrill was and what he had visited the ranch for. He then told him his own private speculations and Farley sat, hands atop the saddlehorn, impassively listening, his long, ruddy face looking darker in shade than in broad day-light. He could have had a little Indian blood in him somewhere, but if he knew this was so he had never mentioned it, and as far as Grant Maxwell was concerned such a thing meant nothing at all.

When Maxwell had said it all, Jess fished out his makings, looped his reins and went to work carefully and thoughtfully, creating a brown-paper smoke. "Gray horse," he said, smoke trailing from his lips, "don't mean much. And if that outlaw was winged down in Fort Collins instead of by you last night—he never could have come this far, if it was the kind of a hurt I figure it's got to be." Jess checked ash and inhaled again, then exhaled. "As for that outlaw not wantin' folks to think he knew the Laramie Plains, hell's bells, Boss, a feller on the run has to be going *some*place, and no matter how it looked to the Pinkerton man, he didn't have to be comin' back up here."

Maxwell said, "There's one thing, Jess. That nickel-plated gun."

"Thirty-eight," shrugged Farley. "I've seen city fellers with them little things tucked under their arms or worn up high, around the same belt that holds up their britches."

"That's the size hole that was in the head of that steer last night," stated Maxwell. "I saw it when one of the boys hoisted the head up for me to see how the steer had been killed. Little round hole much smaller than a six-gun would make, and without the damage to the skull a carbine would make."

Jess took a big drag off his smoke, then smashed the cigarette atop his saddlehorn and flung it away. "That is different," he muttered, very slowly, and raised his eyes. "That is as different as all hell, Boss. And something that's been botherin' me this morning: we should have taken the whole crew and gone back over to that soddy this morning. By now, that rustler can be all the way up to Laramie. Him and his friends."

Grant Maxwell did not agree. "No man would abandon horses like those sorrels, Jess. As for riding over there with the whole crew—they'd see us coming for a mile. If they forted up, we'd be bringing back some empty saddles. I think what we should do is just the two of us ride over there again, in broad daylight."

Farley was agreeable. "When?"

Maxwell looked past where the cowboys were still pushing those anxious cows and their fractious calves and said, "How about right now? Do they need you up here?"

Jess did not bother to look back where the cattle and their drovers were. "No. I sent the other boys farther north to do the same thing. Don't any of them need me."

Grant Maxwell turned his horse and Jess Farley moved out also. Neither of them said much until they were abreast of the village, but about a mile north of it, then Jess wondered aloud if that Pinkerton man was down there, perhaps at the general store, asking questions, and Grant Maxwell thought it was possible.

Across the road, where the free-graze ran for a lot more miles than a man could cover in a hard day of riding, the land was golden and greening up, and empty. There was no movement to be seen until Maxwell and Farley came towards that first soddy, the one where the scrawny woman and the young boy had been the night before. Then, out back by the lean-to, Grant Maxwell saw those two handsome, huge sorrel horses. The big-eyed twelve-year-old was pulling prairie grass and the tame beasts were eating it from his hand. All those big horses had to do was drop their heads and get all the feed they wanted. It was more than just that, and Maxwell understood. So did his rangeboss. The horses were pets, they had probably been hand-raised by someone who never made an angry sound at them. They needed human companionship. Some horses were like that. Not many in the cow country, though.

The sorrels saw both riders before the lad did. By the time he heard shod hoofs rattle over gravelly soil and turned quickly, crouching like a startled deer, the mounted men were between him and the soddy and he could not escape. But he was frightened. Grant Maxwell drew rein. His own son, at this age, had been a head taller. He had also been wilder; Grant could not recall ever seeing his son look at anyone the way this boy was looking up at the two armed, bronzed and unsmiling cowmen. The Lord only knew what tales his parents had told him about cowmen.

Grant smiled. Jess didn't, but then Jess rarely smiled

even when he was in a good mood. The boy said, "They just came over, Mister Maxwell. The big horses, I mean. They just came walking up when I went outside this morning. Maybe they followed someone last night, over in this direction. I didn't coax them."

"They need a friend," said Grant. "They're sure fine animals, aren't they?"

"Yes, sir. My maw said if they was cattle we could live off them for a couple of years, and if we owned a plough and stuff, and a set of harness big enough for 'em, we could surprise my paw when he comes back and have a garden-patch ploughed up and worked down for vegetables."

Maxwell looked beyond, out across the long mile to the place those sorrel horses had come from. It was possible to make out the low roof, and no smoke was coming from the stovepipe. When he looked down again the boy was standing directly in front of one of the sorrels. His head did not reach up to the animal's jaw. The boy said, "If you was going on over there, Mister Maxwell, maybe you could take them along. Those folks might be mad about me petting them, and all."

Grant agreed to that. "All right. They'll follow our horses, I expect. By the way, what's your name?"

"Horace Weatherman. That's my paw's name too." The way the boy pronounced it made it come out 'Horse'.

"Do they call you Horace?"

58

"No, sir. They call me Bud."

Grant nodded as though he liked Bud better. "Tell me something, Bud. Those folks over yonder who own the big sorrel horses—have you seen them up close?"

"Fairly close, Mister Maxwell. Me an' my maw was out hunting berries couple of times and we saw them once, not *real* close, but close."

"What does the lady look like?"

The boy's large eyes were perfectly round. "There isn't a lady. At least, all I saw was three men. Two of 'em got beards and one don't have a beard. My maw says they might be brothers or something, maybe close partners, for otherwise, she says, it don't make a whole lot of sense, them taking up the claim. She says a person who can, ought to hitch up and pull out."

Grant was grave when he said, "Thanks, Bud," and raised his reins to ride on. True enough, the sorrel horses turned and plodded along directly behind the ridden horses.

Jess said, "This is gettin' to smell a little worse all the time," and made a cigarette which he stuck between his lips without lighting it, his full attention fixed coldly and warily upon the hushed, utterly still stretch of onward plain. "You care to bet a half-dollar they didn't run off and leave those big horses, Boss?"

Grant did not reply. They had a good opportunity to study everything that lay ahead of them long before they reached the soddy, and Maxwell noticed two things. One was that shod horses had been bunched up

59

out front of the soddy, probably the night before, or the afternoon of the day before, no earlier than that because the marks were hardly marred at all by the wind and sleet of the previous night.

The second thing he noticed was the soddy's door was open. He turned towards Farley. "Didn't we close that door last night?"

Jess, removing the tie-down from his gun, nodded, unlit cigarette bobbing up and down with this movement. "We closed it. And it had a good hasp, too, so the wind didn't blast it open."

Grant Maxwell thought it possible that the men had returned after he and Farley had been there and had gone. He ranged a probing look farther out. There was another soddy, more westerly than northerly, and off at least one more mile distant. If the men from the soddy in front of him had taken their injured friend over to the farther soddy—why had they done it? Moving a wounded man, particularly on a night as bitter as the previous one had been, wasn't wise even if the situation was desperate.

They halted out front, in plain sight, and dismounted. Grant Maxwell untied his gun, too, then they trooped on over to the ajar door, the only sound being made by their spurs, and, farther back, where one of their horses made a little annoyed squeal at one of the big sorrels, who was nuzzling him.

Grant peeled off his riding gloves, shoved them into the front waistband of his trousers, as was customary, and leaned to push the door open a little wider. A girl no more than sixteen or seventeen leveled a cocked six-gun from the shadows no more than fifteen feet away. She was big-eyed, black-haired, and her face was the color of old snow.

Grant's breath caught up in his gullet. For a couple of seconds no one moved nor spoke, then Grant Maxwell said, "Lady, you don't need that thing. I'm a cowman from over on the far side of Jelm. I'm not here to make trouble for anyone." He saw the finger tighten, and without a wasted motion, dropped down. The sound of a six-gun was loud any time, but cooped up inside four earthen walls, this gun sounded like a cannon. Jess Farley let out a blast of abrupt profanity and hit the door-jamb with his back as the bullet which would have hit Maxwell in the head, angled higher, back where Jess was standing, and tore the crown out of his hat, carrying the headpiece out of the soddy in full flight like a wounded bird.

Grant Maxwell catapulted forward and caught the girl's wrist in an iron grip as she fought with both hands to cock the gun again. He wrenched the Colt out of her hands and pushed her back towards the stove. She spun and lunged for a Winchester that was propped in a corner.

Jess caught her this time, and Jess was not as gentle as his employer had been. He tore the gun away with one hand and sent the girl sprawling with the other hand.

She barely struck the earthen floor than she bounded up spitting like a cougar. The two men were between her and the door, there were no more weapons, evidently—at least, she did not try to get another one—and very slowly all the starch went out of her. She moved heavily towards a chair and sat down, refusing to look up at the cowmen.

Chapter Seven

A STRANGER'S GUN

They couldn't make her talk. Jess said she was the most stubborn single individual he had ever met, and she owed him for a perfectly good Stetson hat, then, as though a near-killing gave him some kind of authorization to do it, Jess went coldly and thoroughly through the soddy making an angry search while his employer stood towering over the girl trying to get responses from her. She sat without raising her face, staring at the earthen floor.

For all her fire and courage she was neither large nor heavy. She was lithe with breasts like oranges, and tan, muscular legs that tapered to fine-boned ankles and small feet. She looked like hundreds of other young girls except that as Grant stood gazing at her, he doubted very much if another young girl would have reacted as this one had. She would have killed him.

Jess returned from his rummaging and handed

Maxwell a tintype he'd found wrapped in a white handkerchief. In this picture a dark-eyed, curly-headed young man was standing beside the same girl who was staring at the floor, only in the picture she was smiling. The young man was strong and vital and young. He had a look of challenge about him and he wore his hat back, his gun tied down, and there was no question about it, he was no squatter.

On the back were the words 'The Kings, Jane and Al, married at Council Bluffs . . .' The rest was too badly smudged to be legible. Grant studied the picture; to a man who remembered things it was possible to understand the girl's small, wonderful smile in the picture, and the young man's look of complete confidence. He and his wife had not posed for a picture when they'd first been married, but he'd seen the same smile on her, and he could remember the same aggressive assurance in himself. But his life, and the life of this young man in the tintype, had taken different forks in the road.

He pocketed the picture and said, "Jane, how bad is your husband hurt?"

It may have been his use of her name or it may have been the mention of the injury, but she lifted her face slowly and looked up at him. "Your kind did it," she said, each word slow-spoken and distinct.

Grant did not offer to argue; he was not an argumentative man. "If they took him to Laramie last night in that storm, it was a foolish thing to do."

She kept staring at Maxwell. "You'd like to know

where they took him, wouldn't you?"

Grant neither agreed nor disagreed. "Laramie isn't that big a town. They can't hide him there very long. Wounded men attract attention."

She drew in a shaky breath and expelled it, then she turned her head slightly and watched Jess Farley at his systematic search. "You're not going to find anything," she told Jess, but he ignored her so she faced Maxwell again. "What gives you the right to break into a squatter's house? You're not the law."

Maxwell said, "No? Who am I?"

The soft mouth, flattened in an ugly and defiant way, sneered. "I know who you are. Maxwell, that rich cowman over beyond Jelm. *They* know who you are, too, and when I tell them you came for Al, they'll look you up, *Mister* Maxwell."

Jess sauntered over and stood, hands in pockets, bitterly regarding the girl. He was silent and that made it worse. Jess was a direct man, uncomplicated and fairly predictable. Finally, he turned and said, "If the detective's still in town we'd better deliver her to him."

Grant Maxwell nodded—but—he had raised a daughter, had watched, wonderingly, while she had made the transformation from a boy-girl to a complete girl. It had been like a miracle to him. His daughter had budded like this one, too, but there it ended. It pained him a little to look at the large gray eyes and the soft mouth and see the first faint showings of hardness there. He'd come here expecting to find only some tracks. He hadn't been at all prepared for this kind of confrontation.

Remembering the Pinkerton detective and his cold, bleak smile did not help much either. He pulled over a chair and sat down. "That gray horse has had a lot of riding," he said. "From the Yellowstone to Fort Collins, then back up here." Jane said nothing; she gave Maxwell stare for stare. He said, "Did your husband know there is a Pinkerton detective tracking him?" The gray eyes flickered with an ancient fear, but that was the only sign she gave that she had even heard. "His name is Verrill and he believes your husband is out here on the Laramie Plains. Jane, this one's nobody's fool, he'll find your man." Maxwell straightened back in the chair as though to rise. "Did you ever see dogs after a wounded wolf? It works the same way with men. Verrill will find him, if not up in Laramie, wherever his friends take him after he's been patched up. Wounded men can't travel fast nor far, but men like that Pinkerton detective never give up."

Farley put in his bit. "And, lady, there are one hell of a lot of those lawmen. Thicker'n fleas on a dog's back."

The flattened mouth loosened a little and Grant saw a quiver, then a swimming brightness to the gray eyes. He sighed, looked up at Jess, then rose heavily and pushed back the chair. "I wish to hell there was some other way," he muttered.

From the door a calm voice said, "There is."

Jess turned, but Grant Maxwell continued to gaze at

the girl a moment longer before he also faced around.

The man in the doorway was bearded, dark-eyed, and sinewy. He was not as tall as either of the cowmen. He had a look of whipcord toughness; he was the kind of a man who never seemed to tire. His age could have been anywhere between twenty-two and thirty-two, the dark beard made him seem older than he actually was. His eyes, though, were young. They were also stone-steady and uncompromising. His cocked Colt had an ivory handle. He was dressed like a rangerider, but that ivory-stocked six-gun implied he was something else even though he had at one time undoubtedly been a cowboy.

"Clean them out," he ordered the girl. "Check that dark one for a knife, he looks like a 'breed. They usually got a hideout in their boot, or somewhere."

The girl rose and mechanically obeyed. She did not look at either Farley or Maxwell as she emptied their hip-holsters, then she made Jess pull his trousers above the boot-tops, but there was no knife, so she stepped almost wearily to the table, put the guns on it, and said, "What are you going to do?" to the man in the doorway.

He did not look at her. "What do you think I'm going to do?"

She said, "No, you're not. Where are the horses?"

"Out back—and your gawd-damned sorrels got to stay. Those are the orders. Walk out of here, Jane."

The girl, smaller than any of them, almost frail-appearing, did not budge. "We go together."

The bearded man finally shot her a flitting, fierce glare. "What are you talking about? Do like you're told; go on out and get in the saddle. I'll be right along."

"No!"

Grant Maxwell was watching the man but listening to the girl. Jess Farley was watching them both. Jess had no feelings, not the way Grant had; he was teetering on the edge of death and knew it, and survival mattered; nothing else did.

"Gunshots can be heard for a couple of miles on a day like this," the girl said. "Like it was said last night, folks are already wondering. You can't do it, or we'll be caught. There's a rope under the bed. I'll cover them while you tie them. Then we can ride out and no one'll pay any attention." The girl paused, her face set in an expression of tough resolution. "How is Al?"

The man in the doorway glared. "No names, you damned fool."

"They know," said the girl. "The biggest one's Maxwell from over beyond Jelm. There's a Pinkerton detective down here looking for Al. Maxwell just told me that." The girl picked up one of the six-guns from the table, cocked it and pointed it at Jess Farley. "Now tie them," she said, spitting out the words.

The man in the doorway reddened. Grant scarcely breathed. Perhaps the girl knew this man well enough to act the way she had, but if she was wrong . . .

The bearded, lithe man slowly lowered his gun, eased down the dog, holstered the thing and stepped briskly around towards the bed behind Jess Farley. He did not say a word but his fury was evident the way he wrenched the knots tight when he tied the cowmen, and when his eyes met Grant Maxwell's gaze, there was death in their dark depths.

When it was done he confronted Maxwell. "Where is this Pinkerton feller?" he growled.

Maxwell replied truthfully. "I don't know. I think he's probably over at Jelm asking questions. He rode into my place at breakfast time this morning on a borrowed horse. Last night I think he was up in Laramie."

"What's his name?"

"Norman Verrill."

The bearded man grunted. "Never heard of him." He turned, his words bitter. "Put the damned gun down, Jane, and let's ride."

The girl lowered the dog, then stood there systematically unloading both weapons. Grant Maxwell watched, admiring two things about her; her calmness and her foresight. The bearded man had not thought unloading the weapons was necessary, but the girl had in mind taking no chances she did not have to take.

Finally, as the man slipped outside and stood looking in all directions, the girl went to the doorway, then faced back, looking straight at Maxwell. "You know where a soft heart will get you someday, Mister Maxwell? Dead!" She whirled and ran out where her companion was.

Maxwell smiled at Jess. "Maybe she's right, but per-

68

sonally, I figure she's wrong. Why did she talk him out of killing us?"

Farley knew what his employer meant, but he did not believe it for one minute, so he answered gruffly. "For the exact reason she give: two gunshots would be heard almost over to Jelm."

Grant shook his head, still smiling. "You know better. You shoot two men down in one of these underground dug-outs, Jess, and if the door was closed no one could hear the sounds fifty feet away."

It was true. Farley thought about and decided that it was true, but he refused to concede that the girl had deliberately saved their lives. Jess went over to the iron stove, backed up to it and began painstakingly to saw the rope holding his wrists behind his back against an edge of rough iron.

Maxwell tried to detect reverberations when the man and girl rode away, but failed. He knew of at least one mistake the girl had made; her picture and the picture of her outlaw-husband was still in Grant Maxwell's pocket.

Farley sawed until perspiration stood out on his face. Maxwell backed up to the water bucket and plunged his bound wrists in and began slowly to work his muscles. It took a long time but eventually the rope yielded as it turned soggy, and in the end Maxwell freed his hands before the rangeboss did. Then he dug out his clasp-knife and set Jess free.

They stood by the table, reloading, saying nothing, and afterwards they went out into the dazzling midmorning sunlight. The change was slightly blinding. Soddies were always dark, morning, noon, and night. Jess picked up his crownless hat, swore and flung it down again.

There was no sighting of the riders, but Grant Maxwell had not expected one. It had taken more than an hour to work free. He turned and saw the big sorrels standing contentedly beside the pair of GM horses; it came back to him what the man had said about having to abandon the girl's sorrels. He already knew someone had raised those huge animals by hand, and that told him a little more about Jane King, the outlaw's wife.

Jess got their mounts and walked back to hand Maxwell his reins. "Tracks are clear enough," said Jess, twisting to point. "West towards the mountains." He dropped his arm. "But that's only for our benefit; they'll head for Laramie, where her husband is."

Maxwell mounted and sat quietly gazing across the empty westerly range. "I don't think so," he ultimately told Farley. "I think west may be their true course, Jess. If they took King to Laramie last night, they got him patched up before dawn. The fact that the one with the ivory-stocked gun arrived like he did makes me think he may have split off from the others and come back for the girl—which I don't think he'd have done if they were running northward or eastward. It'd be too far out of his way."

Jess made a smoke and lit it, letting his narrowed

70

gaze roam far out where the blurry, heat-hazed distant westerly mountains stood. "Maybe we can tell the detective about Laramie, and then when he's gone up there, we could take the boys and scout around to the west."

Grant Maxwell looked at his rangeboss. "You don't like Pinkerton men?"

Farley shrugged. "Never knew one, so I can't like 'em or dislike 'em." Jess exhaled smoke at the sky. "Maybe you were right, in there. Maybe the girl did salvage our hides. I'll tell you, Boss, she's much too young to get shot, and that's the way she's going. Maybe we owe her one."

Maxwell agreed. "All right. You go back to the village and tell the detective they went to Laramie. I'll start trailing them."

"How about the boys?"

"The ranch work comes first. We won't need them anyway, Jess. And seven riders stir up a lot of dust. You and I ought to be able to do this alone, hadn't we?"

Farley looked westerly, looked at his employer, then lifted his reinhand. "Don't see why not. I'll catch up when I can."

They separated out front of the deserted soddy. The big sorrels were in a quandary because they did not know which mounted man to follow, and by the time they had resolved that issue and turned to go after Jess, Farley was spurring his horse in a swift lope towards Jelm and was too far away. The big horses then went plodding back over where the boy had pulled grass for them earlier in the morning.

Chapter Eight

A MATTER OF TRACKING

To read sign on a clear, sparkling day when the ground had been made soft by warmth, was easy. Grant Maxwell rode west and had time to wonder about a few things. One puzzler was how the girl had happened to be in the soddy this morning when her companions had left the night before.

There had been no sign of her the previous night when Grant and Jess had visited the place. Of course, there could have been any one of a dozen reasons. It didn't really matter very much anyway.

Another thing that occupied his thoughts for a while was Jess Farley's easy acceptance of his employer's attitude towards the detective. But that was easier to attribute a reason to; Jess, like most lifelong rangemen, had his own code of justice. He would not have come right out and said he favored tracking down outlaws who had killed a GM beef and the wife of one of whom had very nearly killed him, in order to attend to these things his own way, with a lariat over a tree limb, but that was what it amounted to.

The *legal* kind of law was still weak in a lot of

places, and Wyoming's far plains country was one of them.

Finally, as he kept the trail in front of him, Grant wondered about something he could not resolve quite so readily: if he and Jess caught up with the outlaws, and managed somehow to capture them—what about the girl? It had made him feel old and tired and bad, back at the soddy when Jess had urged him to turn her over to the Pinkerton man, and after she had talked her companion out of a double murder it was even harder to come to a conclusion.

In the end, he put this out of his mind and concentrated upon tracking the pair of shod horses. First things first. The trail was due west. Where it should, by all rights, have veered northward, if that had indeed been the destination of the riders, it did not veer until, another two miles further, it was possible to see the forest-fringe where it closed down closer to the open country, then those tracks changed course, but only very gradually, as though the bearded man with the ivory-stocked gun had a more westerly destination in mind.

Grant Maxwell knew all this country. He had been riding it for a lot more years than he enjoyed recalling. The mountains were interspersed with what were called 'parks', meaning upland meadows, or large glens, some as small as five acres, some as large as several miles across. There was one park, named Shipman's Meadow—after an old-time trapper and hunter who had erected a log cabin up there many years back, and who had subsequently disappeared and no one had ever seen him or heard from him again—which was found to have range cattle in it almost every summer, even though the trail led through a grassless forest and up over timber-line before the descent was begun. Each autumn John Frazier went up there and drove out the mixed brands, got them down to his corrals, and sent word around for the owners to come get their cut-outs.

The lower and nearer meadows, or 'parks', had good grass this time of year and usually a creek passing through them. If a man wanted to lie up for a while, perhaps to allow a wound to heal, any one of the parks would be ideal. There were several that Maxwell knew of where a person could make his camp and watch the entire lower open country, and if he was careful not to send up any smoke during the daylight hours, no one would even suspect he might be up there, until late autumn when the cowmen came up looking for cattle.

It was with this thought in mind that Maxwell finally turned off the trail. He already had estimated its course and knew the onward country well enough to be able to make a fair guess about where those two riders would be going. Southward, farther out into the open country, there was no hiding place. Northward, the mountains were handy and there *were* hiding places, but if there was pursuit, which the girl and her companions would expect, it would be the nearer northward mountains that would be searched first.

Westerly, the mountains ran for many miles. If someone up there had to shift camp he could keep going westward, up one slope and down another, until he was a hundred miles away, and tracking across a thousand-year accumulation of pine and fir needles was not easy, even for an experienced tracker; it was particularly not easy when the people being tracked would be careful about leaving any more sign than they had to leave.

And if they knew he was back there, they would try to ambush him. He already knew one of them, the man with the fancy Colt would kill without a second thought. About the others he could only surmise from what the girl had said. There were more than just her wounded husband and the renegade with the ivory-butted six-gun. That, he was certain of. How many, he had no real idea, but he guessed, from what he remembered of the soddy's interior, that there had to be at least three—and maybe as many as five.

As he studied the onward forest-gloom towards which he was heading, he wondered why only one of those outlaws had been out raiding, leaving his wife and the other outlaws at the soddy. And, of course, there was that original source of bafflement; the puzzler he had tried to figure out the night the steer had been killed: why had a wounded man who was already worn out and within an hour's ride of warmth, safety, and help, stop along the way to try and butcher a steer?

When he reached the trees a big young bull-elk who

had been browsing through a dark thicket suddenly caught the scent of a ridden horse, threw up its large, ugly head, snorted and tried to whirl and bound clear to get running room. Maxwell's gun sprang into his hand and was cocked before the elk broke out and charged like a running horse straight up through the forest.

Maxwell stopped, waited for his heart to settle back, then put up his gun and, looking off in the direction of the elk's noisy flight called the animal a very uncomplimentary name. His horse had not shied, which most horses would have done, but it had all four legs spread stiff, and its eyes wide open and rolling in near-panic.

There were no tracks up in here, but Maxwell had a hunch that sooner or later he would find something even better than shod-horse sign, and he was correct. By staying low, just inside the masking gloom of trees and shadows, he skirted along at a slow gait watching the sun-brightened rangeland out beyond. When he finally saw what he expected to find he stopped and studied both the forward and backward route.

Wagon tires, especially in the spring and early summer when the grass and tiny wild flowers were full of moisture, left a trail a child could follow. If those men up ahead somewhere had put their injured companion upon a saddle animal—but of course if he was badly hurt he'd be unable to sit a saddle, and the fact that he'd managed to hang on as long as he had did not change this; sooner or later, he had to collapse. After that, a wagon was the only way to get him up to

Laramie, and back down to the plains again.

Maxwell did not dwell upon the loyalty of the other renegades towards their friend. If Al King had indeed got as much money as the Pinkerton man implied that he'd got, then it wasn't loyalty with the other outlaws any more than it had been loyalty in the man who had owned that goose that kept laying golden eggs.

The wagon was a light one, judging from the width of the steel tires; probably a ranch-wagon or maybe a spring-wagon. Grant shook his head. Most ranch-wagons did not have springs under them, but even if this one had springs, it would be torture to a sick man to be carted over hard ground through a dark night in a storm.

Perhaps Al King was dead.

Maxwell walked his horse along slowly and quietly. He alternated between watching where the wagon tracks skirted along against the foremost line of big trees, and looking around through the hushed shadows on all sides. If they even thought he was up in here, they would kill him, and he'd never hear the bullet-blast.

Finally, the wagon turned up into the forest. Where this happened there was a wide place. Obviously, the driver had known about this natural causeway, and that meant these outlaws were knowledgeable about the mountains.

Maxwell halted, dismounted, stood gazing at the location of the sun for a while, turned to study the trail taken by the wagon, and decided he had gone about as far as one man ought to go. If Jess hurried, he might be able to track his employer to a rendezvous before sundown; in early summer the light did not fade too swiftly, they way it did in early spring or late winter.

These mountains were full of little veiny creeks that had been cutting deep scars down to bedrock for more centuries than anyone could guess. Some of them would dry up later, when the lower snowfields were dissipated by summer heat, but a great many ran year-round, fed by glacial mountaintops where the snow and ice never completely melted. Maxwell took his horse back to one of these creeks, loosened the cinch and let it tank up. Then he also drank. The water was very cold, but it had a good, fresh taste. It was no substitute for food, though.

He hid the horse and left it tied while he removed his spurs and took along his saddle-gun, but he did not intend to scout the country very far. He had no way of telling how much farther onward the outlaws were. Two things seemed clear enough. One was that those men would have a sentinel up ahead somewhere. The other thing was that, once they felt even reasonably safe, they would stop. Being completely hidden inside a forest, whether it actually meant a man was safe or not, gave that impression. Somewhere, up ahead, at least three men and a girl were camped.

He paralleled the wagon marks for a half-mile and saw where they swung westerly, dipped across a gritty little treeless outcropping, then skidded and bumped their way down into an emerald park where it was easy to see the twin marks all the way across to the far side of the park, and up through the trees again.

He thought they should have stopped in that little park. A flashing, red dagger of sunlight slanting in through lofty treetops, struck something shiny and bounced upwards and outwards, then the flash faded as the treetops cut out the moving sunlight.

Sunlight reflecting off shiny, worn steel wagon tires would look like that. If it *was* the wagon, it had been pulled up through the forest only a short distance past the clearing, perhaps fifty yards or slightly less.

Maxwell crept closer, hugging big trees. There was not a single sign of life in the clearing. He waited, hoping very hard, but whether the wagon indicated that the outlaws had stopped finally, or not, there was no other indication that people had been here.

He pulled back and tried to recall whether there was another park yonder beyond the wagon, but although he knew these mountains well enough, every detail of them was not this clear in his memory. He turned and went back down where he'd left his horse, and beyond that still further until he could see the open range in its fading mantle of red-rusty daylight. There was no sign of Jess anywhere, back eastward.

Chapter Nine

A RENDEZVOUS

The difference between youth and maturity hinges upon judgment; some young men are born with an old rationale, but they are very few in numbers in any age, while older men, through a scaling-down of the actual importance of crises, something which comes, usually at any rate, only with the experience of living, can more often in larger numbers arrive at sound judgments.

That was Grant Maxwell's situation as dusk settled and he saw no sign of Jess Farley. It made very little difference how good a tracker might be, and Farley was as good as any, the simple fact was that after nightfall not even an Indian could have located Maxwell in his forest fastness, unless of course he lit a fire, which he had no intention of doing.

But there were others willing to risk this. He did not see them, or their fire, but he distinctly caught the fragrance and knew, finally, that the renegades were not very far from their wagon, after all.

The temptation to scout was strong, and as the forest gloom gradually deepened Maxwell eventually yielded to it. His horse was too distant to smell those other horses and nicker, the darkness would be his constant ally, and with visibility limited the sentinel those men would have had out watching earlier, would probably by now have gone back to eat with the others.

Reaching the park where he had seen the wagon tracks earlier required nothing more than cautious, silent circling out and around, staying among the fringe of trees, and the matter of locating that secret camp was made easy by the wood-fire scent. When it grew vague he altered course, when it was strongest he moved towards it. If there had been wind he would have had a problem, but this night, at least in the forest, it was as hushed and still as it could be.

Time in a forest, even at midday, was something a man had to think about to be aware of. At night, Maxwell had no more than a very vague inkling how long it took him to press onward until, ultimately, the scent of firewood was followed by a glimpse of orange light through the trees beyond the park.

He crested another low land-roll, like the previous one, consisting of a barren outcropping of scabby rock, and saw the camp.

There *was* a second clearing, smaller than the previous one. The fire was in the grass near the western, curved side of the little glen, and although Maxwell lay prone, like a skulking Indian, studying each detail, he could not make out exactly how many people were down there because the fire was confined and kept small.

The smell of food was a distraction. Maxwell had

not eaten since morning, but it was never a serious distraction; day-long hunger paled when a man's life was at stake.

He saw one slight person rise and go back beyond the nearest trees and thought he recognized the girl. Otherwise, he lay there longer than prudence dictated in order to try and ascertain whether there were four men at the fire or five. He never did make this determination. When he slid back and rose to return to his horse he was only certain of two things: he knew where the outlaws were, and there were more than three of them.

When he got back to his horse Jess was standing there, watching his approach without even a gun in his hands. Maxwell was relieved. "How did you find me?" he asked, and Farley fished out some tinned beans with pork and handed them over as he gravely replied:

"I didn't, my horse did. He whinnied and your horse answered. Only I didn't know it was your horse until I got up here."

They sat down to eat and Maxwell told Farley all he knew, all that he had recently seen. The rangeboss, squatting cross-legged with his hat shoved back and his face looking longer and thinner in the gloom, listened without interrupting. Then he said, "Well, that damned Pinkerton feller didn't go up to Laramie like he was supposed to." Jess masticated thoroughly before explaining. "And he was mad. Said we knew all along where them people was, which I said was a damned lie, and maybe we'd have tangled except that Ellis Burton, from the store, and three, four other fellers in the saloon where I found the Pinkerton feller, got between us." Farley tipped back his head, lifted the tinned beans and let about a third of the food slide into his mouth, then he lowered his head and methodically chewed again before continuing.

"He was trying to borrow or hire a horse when I left Jelm. Old Burton wouldn't let him use his plug again, which was probably all for the best; that damned critter was born the same year I was. This kind of riding would kill him. Anyway, come morning we'd ought to catch sight of Verrill somewhere down my backtrail. I drifted up into the trees as soon as I could."

Maxwell nodded; this, then, was the reason he had not seen Farley.

"But that feller's no greenhorn. He'll pick up the trail come sunup." Farley finished his tin of beans. "If there are four or five of those boys up ahead, maybe we could stand Mister Pinkerton's company until the smoke clears . . . If you got in mind jumping them before sunup."

Maxwell had not actually formulated a plan. Until Jess's arrival he had been thinking defensively. He also finished his tin and dug a little hole in the pine needles to bury it, which really was no more than a token gesture because the first four-footed little varmint like a raccoon or a porcupine that picked up the scent would dig it up.

Jess made a cigarette and would have lit up except

that Grant Maxwell scowled, so Jess sat there with the unlit thing between his lips and said, "I've been over in here a few times, in the fall of the year, and damned if I can think how they're going to be able to keep going with that wagon."

Maxwell had already thought about this. "They'll either abandon it, or else they'll have to drop back to the open country southward and skirt along the edge of the trees. A forest makes a pretty good background, if you stay close to it."

Jess did not dispute this, but he said, "Wagons leave pretty clear sign this time of year. I wonder, if they knew they was being trailed, how long it'd be before they'd prop that King feller against a damned tree and take to their heels on horseback?"

Maxwell thought that would depend on how many men they thought were trailing them. "The two of us aren't going to scare them very much. Even with the Pinkerton man, it isn't going to look like a very big posse."

That made Farley's thoughts go back and he wagged his head. "You know, Boss, that feller would be downright dangerous if he decided he didn't like someone."

Maxwell said, "Glad you noticed," and picked up a dry pine needle to use as a toothpick. "While you were in town, did he try and recruit a posse, by any chance?"

Farley didn't know. "I left while he was still damning you up one side and down the other side. I don't know. But if he did I can predict he isn't going to have much success. It don't set too well with folks to have a plumb stranger drift in and right away start bad-mouthing someone folks been putting store in for a lot of years." Jess pulled out his six-gun and gravely examined it, then shoved it back and settled his wide, lean shoulders against a big tree. "I got to thinkin' on the ride out here: these outlaws got to be real professionals. If King got as much cash as it seems likely he got, and there are another three or four of those fellers, just as good as King, they must have one hell of a lot of money with them. Unless they maybe buried it back at the soddy, and if it'd been me I'd have dug it up last night and hauled it along with me." Farley looked from beneath his down-swooping hat-brim. "Suppose they got a couple of saddlebags full of greenbacks, and suppose we are able to corral them, and suppose we hand everything over to that Pinkerton feller; I've heard of some pretty trustworthy men bein' overwhelmed by a big pile of free money."

Theorizing was something men did in the gloaming upon the front porch, maybe with a glass of whisky in their hands after supper. Grant Maxwell was not given much to speculations under circumstances like the one he was now involved with, so he said, "Let's worry about keeping a whole skin first, and about our chances of sneaking over there after midnight and trying to get some ropes on those outlaws. The Pinkerton man can wait."

Jess thought that over. "Pretty damned big odds," he

muttered. "You didn't live this long taking chances like that."

Maxwell smiled. Jess was too old to be Maxwell's son; he could have been his *brother* though, and this was the kind of relationship they had evolved over the years. They were frank with one another and, at times, like now, skeptical of one another's judgments.

"Jess, sure as hell as that detective comes loping along on your backtrail in the morning, they are going to see him—and *that* puts you and me between hell and a hot place, doesn't it? So—we can go on back, or we can take a chance. I'll leave it up to you."

Farley pondered. "How many did you say there was?"

"I'm not sure, but at least four. Not counting the girl."

Jess snorted. "You'd better count her. I'd say she'd be quicker to shoot a man than most men. You know where I got this hat? Bought it at the general store and it cost me five dollars. That one she ruint only cost four dollars and it was a better hat. Three X beaver, Stetson. Ellis Burton said I must have bought it ten years ago; prices have gone up that much in just ten years. You'd better count the girl, which makes five, and if there's another one . . . Boss, suppose we go back, or wait for the detective. Two men, even skulkin' up on them in the night, don't stand too good a chance of walking away afterwards. Those are damned awful odds; I'd never bet money on them in a crap game. I should have gone back to the ranch and brought on the whole crew."

Maxwell agreed. "Bad odds, Jess, but I didn't have in mind making a clean sweep. Maybe we can get the wounded one and the girl. But what we really ought to be able to do without a whole lot of danger is stampede their stock."

Slowly, very gradually, Farley's gloom lifted. "Yeah. I wasn't thinking of that. We can set them afoot. Say! We might even be able to make off with them saddlebags."

Maxwell thought otherwise. "You don't believe they'd hang them on a tree limb like just an ordinary set of bags, do you? We'd better forget that money, Jess; they'll be sleeping atop it four deep, and I wouldn't bet they don't have someone sitting up with a gun even though they probably don't believe anyone can get close until tomorrow. Let's just concentrate on the wounded man, the girl, and their horses."

Jess removed his unlit smoke and flung it away. "Maybe just the horses, Boss. That wounded feller's probably not sleeping much, and the girl won't be either, if she's looking after her man. Suppose we just concentrate on the horses. I'll tell you why—that wounded feller isn't going anywhere on foot; we can probably grab him in the morning—and his wife."

Grant yawned and considered Farley's plan, and decided in the end that it was soundly based and was better than his own suggestion. He nodded and said, "Just the horses." He cocked an eye upwards through the topmost treetops. It looked much later than it actually was; it looked dark enough to be midnight, but he guessed it to actually be no more than perhaps nine or ten o'clock, which was late enough by range standards. If he and his rangeboss had been at home on the ranch, by now they both would have been fast asleep.

He rose, picked up his carbine, and waited until Jess had also unwound up to his full height. "Stay close, and if there's trouble, try and get back here to the horses." He waited for some kind of comment, but Farley offered none, but he looked meaningfully at the saddlegun. Maxwell had picked the weapon up unconsciously. Now, though, he interpreted his rangeboss's expression correctly: this would not be a long-range battle, if it came to a battle. In a forest in the darkness a Colt would be all he'd really need.

He went over to shove the Winchester back into its saddleboot, then they left the relative safety of their hiding place and, with Grant Maxwell leading, headed back around the first park towards the bony outcropping that overlooked the second park.

Maxwell had seen the horses grazing beyond the little supper fire in that second meadow, but had scarcely heeded them. Now, he tried to recall their approximate location, and gave it up as he and Jess began the ascent towards the second outcropping. No matter where grazing horses had been an hour or two earlier, it was not reasonable to expect them to still be in the same place. It didn't matter anyway; the horses would be wherever they now were, and Maxwell with Jess Farley would have to make their impromptu plans accordingly.

Chapter Ten

SUCCESS

They reached the second glade despite the darkness and the very impaired visibility. There were embers glowing where the cooking fire had died down, but they did not help at all.

A man's eyes became accustomed to darkness, but only up to a point, after that it was impossible to be sure of anything.

Maxwell remained a long time in one spot where he could see several lumpy shapes, but unless he knew how many outlaws there were it did not help much to be able to make out what looked like four or five people in bedrolls in the vicinity of the fire.

Jess leaned close and whispered something about this. Maxwell nodded without replying, and began a careful advance around through the trees at the edge of the glade. If he had to abandon his idea of capturing the wounded man and perhaps the girl, he would do it without much regret, providing he could stampede the horses. As Jess had said, it amounted to the same thing; once the outlaws were afoot they would have no way to transport the injured man.

Eventually, he found the horses. What made that possible was the gray animal. He alone, of what looked like six or seven animals over towards the west side of the glade, showed up in the weak starshine reaching down into the clearing.

For a moment Maxwell stood watching, then he ducked his head and said, "Hobbled." Farley nodded; he too had noticed that each time a horse moved, out there, it reared back its head and hopped with both front feet in the air at the same time.

Of course, this increased the risk; it took an extra few minutes to approach horses, especially when the men were strange to the animals, and especially in the night, to get close enough to bend down and unbuckle hobbles.

Jess sighed and Grant Maxwell turned to whisper. "Stay back here and cover me. I don't see anyone, but if one of those animals snorts or makes a fuss it's going to rouse the camp."

Jess stood gazing out where the horses were peacefully cropping rich meadow grass. He did not look encouraged by this most recent development, but he did not try and dissuade Maxwell.

There was one advantage to being unable to see very far. Neither could the outlaws see very far, if it came to that. Maxwell motioned for Jess to stay where he was, then started a little onward scout, alone. He did not believe there was a guard, but he had to be sure.

He went on around the clearing, part way, bearing

northerly, then on around northeasterly, covering perhaps a hundred yards, then he turned back having seen nothing that resembled a man hunkering in the shadows with a blanket round his shoulders. When he found Farley, he nodded as though to imply it was safe to leave the forest, turned out past the last trees and moved silently out in the direction of the horses.

At once, a hobbled horse either saw movement or scented a man and threw up its head. This was a big, line-backed dun horse, powerfully set up, evidently spooky. Maxwell halted. Under normal conditions he would have talked his way up to this horse, but tonight he could not make a sound, so he and the line-backed dun stared at one another.

Another horse, then a third one, detected the presence of a man and also flung up their heads. Maxwell was now committed; but it also happened that Grant Maxwell was a lifelong horseman. He knew instinctively that if he approached the snorty dun, the animal was going to whirl and excite the other horses, so he moved sideways towards the next nearest animal. That one, too, sucked back and extended its nostrils, ready to emit a loud snort of fear. Maxwell bypassed that one as well. It was the gray horse with the visible, strange brand on his left shoulder that watched Maxwell's approach without stiffening. This was the horse stolen over along the Yellowstone river; it was by now not only accustomed to strange men, it had also been ridden hard enough over the past week or two so that it did not have much fire left in it.

Maxwell got right up beside the gray, got a hand upon its neck, patted it and ran the hand down the neck to the shoulder, then on down lower to the pastern, and when the gray stood as docile as a setter pup, Maxwell groped for the buckle and worked off the hobbles.

But he did not release the gray. When he straightened up he slipped the hobbles around the horse's neck and turned him very gently, leading him up beside the next horse, an act which made his strange presence a lot less objectionable to the nearest mount. In this way he removed hobbles from three horses. But he could not get close to the line-backed dun. In the end he gave up on that one and set another horse free. Then a very strong premonition made him squat low in the darkness with the horses all around him, and peer in the direction of the camp.

Maybe it hadn't been a premonition; maybe, as he squatted in front of each horse concentrating on removing the hobbles, he had heard a sound that did not register right away.

There was a man, hatless and motionless, over in the direction of the camp, standing where it was barely possible to make out his silhouette. He was gazing in the direction of the horses. Maxwell knew that up until now the horses had not been acting normally, something any horseman would recognize at once, but at least the animals had not made any noise, and that might mitigate what lookcd to Maxwell to be interesting the bareheaded outlaw.

If the man had a gun, Maxwell could not make it out, and conversely, as long as Maxwell stayed low against the ground with the horses around him, that outlaw over there would be equally as incapable of seeing Maxwell.

Finally, the outlaw expectorated, scratched his ribs and turned back. Maxwell began to breathe again. Of course, if trouble had come, that outlaw was as good as dead, but that was a lot less important than not having to kill the man, and letting things go on quietly.

But Maxwell was finished. He did not try to approach the dun, or that other snorty horse. He had freed four and would have liked to try for one more, but one warning was enough; moreover, there were only three horses still hobbled and two of them were wagon animals. Maybe they were combination horses—broke to ride and drive—but this was not necessarily so; many driving horses knew nothing about carrying people on their backs and objected when someone tried to straddle them. But whether this was so or not, what really mattered was that now the outlaws had three horses for four or five people.

Maxwell kept his hold of the docile gray, rose on the far side of it, waited what seemed like half the night but which was no more than five minutes, then he began to very stealthily lead the gray, with the other loose horses following.

He got southward to the edge of the trees, and Jess was waiting down there, like an apparition, to help.

They took the freed horses a hundred yards south-ward, near the open range beyond, turned them loose and flung clods after them. The horses started towards the open country. Back in the park one of the remaining hobbled horses whinnied loudly; evidently a horse among the escaping animals was this squealing animal's partner and he did not like the sep-aration. He called twice, then Maxwell and Farley could hear him coming, hopping frantically in the direction his friend had taken. Some experienced horses could hop faster with their forelegs hobbled than a man could run. As Maxwell jerked his head and set a fast pace, heading back the way he had come, he hoped this hobbled horse would be one of those expe-rienced animals. If he was, then the outlaws would have only two horses left.

He and Farley were nearing the rearward outcrop-ping when a fierce outburst of profanity back in the direction of the outlaw encampment told the story, and Jess paused to look back and say, "Well, there goes any idea you had of getting the wounded feller and his wife. We'd better get the hell out of here, Boss. Those fellers are going to be swarming through these trees like hornets in another few minutes, and come day-light they'll know damned well them horses didn't unbuckle all those hobbles themselves."

Other angry outbursts back down in the far park rose up loudly as Maxwell led the way back to where he and Jess had left their horses.

It did not take long to get mounted. Maxwell led off

down through the trees towards the open country, then he turned west for a short distance until they ran out of trees. Ordinarily he would never have gone out of the forest, but the darkness was a fair substitute, and what he wanted to do next was make certain that those freed horses did not allow themselves to be caught. Jess grunted as they put the forest at their backs. It could have been a sound of disapproval, or it could have been a grunt of dismay, but since Jess did not speak and Maxwell did not encourage him to, they passed southward for about a quarter of a mile, until Maxwell felt sure no one could spot them, then he swung west again heading up in the direction of the loose stock.

Jess was far more interested in the northerly ring of trees than he was in the onward range country, and for a most excellent reason: somewhere up there furious outlaws, like rabid dogs, were looking for their lost animals. They would be armed and deadly, and Jess Farley had no wish at all to be skylined as he rode across an area that was absolutely devoid of cover.

Grant Maxwell alternated; he tried to detect sound or movement up where the loose stock was, and he also kept a wary eye towards the rim of trees beyond which was a solid, impenetrable blackness.

Finally, it was the gray again that helped. He alone of the animals that had been freed, stood out. The other horses were solid colors, bays, browns, chestnuts, shades that blended very well with the night.

Except for one animal, the spooky line-backed dun horse still wearing his hobbles, the little remuda was drifting farther out over the range, southward. Maxwell's idea was to facilitate this southward movement; if he had been able to discern that gray, as soon as the outlaws ran down out of the trees they would very likely be able to make him out too. Maxwell motioned for Jess to follow, turned slightly towards the trees to get behind the horses, and when this had been accomplished, he turned suddenly southward. So did Jess. At once the loose stock sighted or scented their drovers and moved off, not fast but warily and briskly. For a little distance the snorty dun horse could keep up, but eventually, when Maxwell was reasonably certain he and Jess were beyond sight of anyone in the forest and whipped up the loose horses into a lope, the line-backed dun fell back. He could hop very well, though. Grant took down his rope, urged his mount in from the right, and roped the dun. At once the snorty horse set back and refused to budge. He was rope-wise. While Maxwell kept the lariat taut, Jess dismounted and removed the dun's hobbles. Then he freed the big, stout animal from Maxwell's lariat, and with a great squeal the dun raced away into the night looking for his friends.

At the same time someone back in the trees cut loose with a carbine and Jess vaulted into his saddle, hooked his horse and kicked up a shower of dirt and grass as he fled westward beside Grant Maxwell.

The man with the Winchester could not have seen

them out there freeing the dun, but whatever had inspired him to try a blind shot would have been entirely unimportant if he'd hit someone. As every rangeman knew, being killed or badly wounded by accident was not one damned bit less final or painful than being shot on purpose.

They did not haul up for a full mile. Then Jess stepped down, put his ear to the ground, got up with a head-wag, indicating that he could not detect the sound of those fleeing freed horses, and fished forth his makings to roll a smoke. This one he could light behind his hat and smoke as they rode onward.

Grant Maxwell studied the black-hulking westerly and southwesterly mountains. He told Jess that if those outlaws knew the countryside as well as he felt they did, their course would have to be in one of two directions.

"Onward, the way they were heading, or upland, in a northerly direction, and also westerly. They need horses, but when they find our sign—which they will come sunup—they won't head back eastward towards Frazier's corrals. They'll know someone is on their trail. Northwesterly or due west they have a lot of rough country to pass through, and before they can go out on a raiding expedition they've got to hide their gear and their money."

Jess smoked and kept looking back as he said, "There ain't any cow camps westerly for more than a hundred miles. *North*westerly they could find a camp or two, with horses." Jess dropped the smoke and trampled it, then he got back astride as he said, "You know, when that bastard cut loose back there I think I shrank two inches. I was just lookin' at my shadow. It's shorter than it was."

Maxwell laughed, Jess almost grinned, and they rode on.

Chapter Eleven

IN BROAD DAYLIGHT

Grant Maxwell had done this before. Not *exactly* the same thing, but a fair approximation of it. And he'd had bronco bucks do it to him: stalk and maneuver, back and fill, jockey and fade back.

He was perfectly satisfied those outlaws would not take the wounded man. Normally, they might have forced his wife to accompany them, but not when it would require taking her up behind someone's cantle, when there was pursuit somewhere around.

He and Jess stopped once to let their horses graze for a couple of hours. That was before daybreak. After first light they got back astride. Maxwell had a very dangerous game in mind; the outlaws needed horses desperately. Maxwell and Jess Farley had a pair of horses. Probably the only horses within miles. Maxwell kept moving, kept picking his way silently and dangerously close, leaving fresh horse sign as he went, his idea being that if he could keep the attention of the outlaws he could delay them.

But it only worked that way for a short while, after sunup, then, as Grant and Jess sat upon an uphill ledge watching, the trackers gave up and hurried back towards their little park beyond the wagon. Maxwell led off down through the forest and Jess followed. Where they stopped the next time was out of sight of the park but well within hearing distance. Men were cursing as they saddled up. Maxwell dismounted to go closer, then halted suddenly, where he could see into the park. Jess almost walked up on to his heels as Maxwell suddenly turned and hastened back. Jess followed again, but looking perplexed.

When they got back Maxwell wasted no time getting into the saddle and heading northwesterly deeper into the forest. Where he halted, finally, a mile off, Jess said, "What spooked you?"

Maxwell kept watching the rearward forest. "What did you see out there, Jess?"

"Three fellers saddling three horses."

Maxwell smiled. "There should have been more men out there." He turned to continue probing the rearward forest. "We damned near did it that time."

Farley rubbed his scratchy jaw. "A trap? Well, well, those boys are pretty enterprisin', I'd say."

They rode on, still westerly, and eventually drifted down towards the edge of the forest to look out over the open range. Three horses bearing heavy burdens were about a quarter-mile out into the new-day sunshine.

Maxwell was concentrating on those fleeing men when Jess gave one of his grunts and pointed almost due east, back along the line of merging forest and plain. A horseman was clearly visible coming westerly. Jess spat and reached to make a smoke. "What in hell took him so long? Those Pinkerton fellers must sleep late in the morning." Jess lit up.

Maxwell watched, and appreciated that very shortly now Norman Verrill was going to see the escaping outlaws. Whether he thought they actually *were* outlaws or not wasn't too important, because the outlaws were also going to see—not Norman Verrill, especially—but someone riding a *horse*.

He said, "This ought to be interesting," and rested both hands atop the saddlehorn, waiting for Verrill to cover another few hundred yards and discern the outlaws. Out there, southward and on an angling westerly course, the outlaws, with perhaps more reason to be vigilant, saw Verrill first and stopped in a bunch.

About this time the Pinkerton detective caught sight of those horsemen. He was, Maxwell thought, too distant to make out the fact that the outlaws were for the most part riding double, but even as Maxwell had this thought he saw bright sunlight flash off metal, and because it was much too far for Verrill to be drawing a gun, the detective had to be lifting a spyglass to his eye. Farley said, "What's he doing, can you make it out?"

Maxwell said what he thought, and Jess pondered that for a while. As Verrill suddenly changed course to leave the fringe of forest, heading southwesterly in the direction of the outlaws, Jess said, "Those fellers must travel pretty well equipped, havin' a spyglass and all," then, as he continued to follow the detective's course, he added another little, very dry observation. "And if he don't haul up darned soon someone out there with a Winchester is going to knock him out of the saddle."

Maxwell silently agreed, but he had more confidence in Verrill, whom he had met, and who had impressed Grant Maxwell as being anything but a careless or foolish man.

"He'll haul up, Jess."

Verrill did, and just beyond what Maxwell carefully estimated to be only a few yards beyond Winchester range. He and the outlaws sat out there in brilliant sunlight gazing at one another. Then an outlaw raised his hand, palm forward, turned his horse and began a slow walk towards the detective. This outlaw was not carrying an extra man behind him on the horse's back.

Jess exhaled smoke, looking as though he relished being a spectator. "You know, Boss, I've heard some of those fellers who carry them little revolvers on their trouser-belts can draw them pretty fast. It's beginning to look like I'm going to find out if that's true."

But it did not happen that way because Verrill calmly unshipped both feet, slid to the ground, turned his horse so that its barrel was between the oncoming

101

outlaw and himself. He was too distant for either Maxwell or Farley to see whether he had a pistol resting upon the saddleseat, but that was customary when a man acted as Verrill had just acted.

The outlaw stopped suddenly and sat a moment. Maybe he could see a gun and maybe he couldn't, but he too knew what that kind of a maneuver meant. Moments later he turned and walked his horse back to his waiting friends. The band of them remained stationary and huddled, probably talking, for another short while before one of them turned west and led off back towards the forest, but it was at least two miles distant in that direction now, and the others followed him.

Verrill did not mount up again. He remained out there watching the burdened horses for quite some little time, then he got back astride and instead of going after the outlaws, he turned northward, heading for the part of tree-gloom where Maxwell and Farley sat.

Jess killed his smoke atop the saddlehorn and said, "Now what? Go back and look for the wounded feller and the woman?"

Maxwell nodded without speaking. He was watching Norman Verrill. He did not anticipate this meeting with any illusions, and when the detective was close enough to catch movement, Maxwell urged his horse out, just beyond the last row of trees, and signaled with an upraised arm.

Verrill did not halt, but while his horse kept plodding along he slipped his right hand inside his coat and kept it there until, something like seventy or eighty yards away, he recognized Maxwell. Then he withdrew the hand.

Jess eased forward too. When the detective rode on up he looked with candid hostility from one rangeman to the other, let his glare linger finally upon Grant Maxwell and said, "Did you get your share?"

Maxwell did not take umbrage. "Only in horses," he replied calmly. "We ran off four of their animals. That's why you saw them riding double."

Verrill continued to look hostile. "There's a law against what you did, Mister Maxwell. It's called aiding and abetting criminals."

Maxwell's tone of voice did not change, but his words were slightly sharper. "Think what you like, Mister Verrill." He turned his horse and headed back in the direction of the outlaw encampment. Jess turned back too. Verrill sat a moment, then kneed his horse out as he said, "What are you going up in there for; those men are riding west."

Farley answered. "Not all of 'em."

Grant Maxwell took no chances. He had few doubts about the injured outlaw being back in the forest, somewhere close to the outlaw camp, and he had even less reason to believe that if the outlaw saw three strangers coming towards him, he would not try to shoot them. Then there was the girl. He already knew first-hand what she was capable of.

They left the horses in a clump of trees and went

onward afoot with Norman Verrill saying nothing, his face still dark and stormy.

Maxwell got atop the little shale outcropping above the second park and lay prone to wait for movement somewhere down below and out across the meadow. There was no one near where the camp had been, but there were several saddles and a tangle of bridles and bedrolls and other equipment lying down there, abandoned.

Jess reached, touched Maxwell's arm, and pointed, all without uttering a sound. Grant Maxwell followed out a sighting along his rangeboss's arm and saw the girl standing just inside a depth of tree-shadows over across the meadow, westward. Behind her, only partially visible, was a scrap of something gray-white and lumpy, low against the ground. Norman Verrill started to raise up and Maxwell flung over an arm to hold the detective still.

"Don't move," he hissed. "She's doing exactly what we're doing. Waiting to catch sight of something moving."

Verrill froze in position.

The girl stood like that for a long time before turning to step back deeper into the gloom and kneel beside the lumpy thing on the ground. As soon as her back was to him Grant Maxwell pushed back and got upright. He knew his way around the clearing, to the left. He had already made that trip once, in the pitch darkness. This time, as he led off, he looked back at the detective. "Jess isn't going to give us away, and neither am I. It's up to you."

Verrill gave a sulky nod of understanding, and followed along.

They made slow progress, but then there was no reason for haste. They were as silent as wraiths. Maxwell went deeper down, this time, too, until they had to start their turn towards the northerly course closer to where the wounded man was lying and where the girl was staying close to him.

From this point on Maxwell halted every few steps. The forest was dark and cool here. It was also thick enough with giant trees to limit visibility to only a few yards. The last thing Grant Maxwell wanted was to be seen before he was ready to be seen. Jess and the detective walked crouched and Verrill had a gun in his hand.

Maxwell came up behind a giant bull-pine, halted and gradually peered around it. He saw the wounded man lying on his back not more than a hundred feet ahead, but there was no sign of the girl. That worried him. She would be armed, he knew that instinctively. He eased back and turned to throw a probing look behind and off on both sides, but wherever she was, either she was standing perfectly still, or else she was out of sight among the trees. He and Jess exchanged a look. Jess shrugged and showed his six-gun, but he did not draw back the hammer. Even that little grating sound would carry as far as where the wounded man was lying. The forest was as hushed as death; there were no squirrels and no birds to scold.

The girl suddenly appeared off on Maxwell's left. He caught the blur of movement and flashed his right hand downward and upward, gun in hand, as he swung his head.

She had seen the three of them, but the shock had momentarily paralyzed her. Then, as Jess started to move, Maxwell saw the gun swing and he called out to her.

"Don't do it, Jane!"

Maxwell did not aim at the girl, he swung his six-gun towards the wounded man as he cocked it. The girl saw, and understood. She had her weapon pointed at Jess Farley. He seemed to be holding his breath. Verrill, too, was rigid. Only Maxwell was calm enough to make an objective study of the girl's tight-taut face. He did not expect her to pull that trigger, but there was always the chance. Especially with a woman.

Seconds dripped by in absolute silence. Maxwell did not speak again because there was nothing to say; whatever happened next was up to Jane King.

She lowered the tip of her pistol barrel very slowly at first, then she let the full weight of the heavy six-gun drag her arm down.

From out beyond the bull-pine where the wounded man lay, a husky, fading voice said, "Jane . . . ? What is it, Jane?"

She did not answer. She lowered the hammer on the six-gun and lifted her gray eyes to Grant Maxwell. She looked beaten.

Chapter Twelve

THE STILLNESS, FINALLY

The outlaw had a carbine lying beside him on one side, a six-gun within easy reach on the other side, but he made no move towards either weapon, and when Grant Maxwell was close enough to look into the outlaw's gray face he thought privately that the outlaw could not have lifted the six-gun, let alone the Winchester. He looked to be about one breath away from expiring. His eyes drifted aimlessly and his lips were cracked and bone-dry.

The girl was between Jess and Verrill when they too walked on up. She sank to her knees beside the wounded man, shoulders bowed, hands lying like dying birds.

Maxwell thought she would dissolve with tears, but instead she lifted a hand and smoothed back the wounded man's curly hair and said, "It's all over, Al. Two of these are the cowmen I told you we left tied back at the soddy." Her voice quavered at the end and she drew back her hand very gently.

Maxwell sank to one knee and raised the dirty old army blanket that covered the outlaw. He was shirtless. There was a thick, professional-looking bandage around his lower middle, and a second bandage up higher. Both had dark blood showing through. Maxwell lowered the blanket gently as Norman Verrill stooped and swept up the carbine and handgun beside the injured man. He very methodically unloaded both weapons, then tossed them over against the foot of a big pine tree.

He said, "You're Al King," to the wounded man. If it was a question, it did not sound like one. It sounded like a statement. The outlaw looked long at Verrill, then, without answering, he let his head loll back and he closed his eyes.

Jess said, "Anyone got any whisky?"

No one had. The girl looked at Grant Maxwell's grave face, and swallowed. "It was you that ran off the horses, wasn't it?"

Grant looked across at her and nodded. "They'd have killed him trying to go any further. We did you a favor."

The outlaw spoke without opening his eyes. "That was—no favor, Cowman. The law wants—me."

Verrill spoke up. "For robbery and murder, King. They want you in Idaho, in Wyoming, and in Colorado."

Jess growled the Pinkerton man into silence by saying, "Leave it be. He's not going anywhere. You can tell him all the bad news later." Before Verrill could reply, Jess then said, "Boss, I can hustle back for a team to put on that wagon in the trees, and we can get him back to Jelm or to the ranch by nightfall."

Grant Maxwell said nothing. He had seen a lot of

injured men in his lifetime. He had seen men die from loss of blood before; this one had all the signs. There were only two things in his favor; he was young, and the girl was there to watch over him. The ride back to the ranch would certainly start the bleeding all over again, and judging from the outlaw's weakened condition he had already lost a lot of blood from the same kind of jarring up to Laramie and back down here, in a wagon.

Maybe he had enough blood left to pull through, but hauling him another dozen and more miles would most certainly change that.

Maxwell said, "All right, Jess. Also, bring back the riding crew."

Verrill's face darkened with instant suspicion. "What do you need with more men, Maxwell?"

Grant looked up, his patience with the Pinkerton man just about at the end of its tether. "Unless you want to track down those other outlaws alone, Verrill," he said, in a restrained, hard tone, "We'll need more than just what we now have."

Verrill subsided, and his expression loosened a little. But Jess, as he rose and dusted his knees, seemed not exactly to approve of leaving Maxwell there with Verrill. "I could take the detective back with me," he said to his employer, without so much as looking at Verrill, who glared at him.

Grant shook his head. "No need, Jess. Just fetch back a team and the boys. We'll all be here just like we are now, when you get back."

Finally, Farley straightened up and turned to put a sulphurous, dark-eyed look at the Pinkerton man. It was less a threatening glance than it was a promising one.

After Jess had departed Maxwell shed his coat. It was gradually turning quite warm in the forest, which meant that by now it was downright hot out upon the plains.

He sent the girl for some water at the creek, and Verrill went tramping along, following her out and back, something that made Maxwell's jaw ripple, but he said nothing.

They removed the top blanket and used a soiled rag to dampen the wounded man's upper body. Evaporating water made a person feel cool when the heat was increasing in the stillness where the outlaw lay.

King opened his eyes, studied Verrill, studied Grant Maxwell, and said, "You fellers figure to haul me back in the wagon?"

Verrill said, "Yes," and Maxwell said, "No." The outlaw flicked a glance back and forth. So did his wife, who was very tenderly wiping his face with a wet rag.

Grant did not look at the detective. "When you're able to make it, we'll haul you back. Until you're able, you'll stay right here."

The outlaw concentrated on Maxwell, and the cowman, who still had that tintype of those two young people in his pocket, thought that somewhere between Fort Collins and this gloomy forest Al King had lost

110

that arrogant, challenging look. Now, he looked a lot younger, a lot less yeasty. It was Grant Maxwell's private opinion that when they finally loaded Al King into the wagon for the trip back, the outlaw would be dead.

Verrill did not challenge what Maxwell had said. He stood there above the outlaw looking down at him, his cold, pale eyes speculative and dispassionate. He said, "The way I got it, King, they only shot you once down at Fort Collins."

The outlaw closed his eyes again. His chest rose and fell in a fluttery, fading way. "They did. The wound up through the shoulder. It—slowed me down—but after a while it went numb. It wasn't no forty-five slug, anyway. It was from some little pistol—small-caliber slug."

"Where'd you get the lower-down wound then?" Verrill asked, and before the outlaw could answer Grant Maxwell did that for him.

"I gave it to him night before last during the storm." The outlaw opened his eyes and stared. Maxwell said, "When you were trying to carve off a haunch of that steer of mine you shot."

King kept staring at Maxwell.

The girl looked over too, her gray eyes dry and hard. Maxwell's gaze did not waver, but right at this moment he did not feel proud of himself; the dead steer kept looking less and less significant.

He said, "What in the hell made you try and haul off some beef when you were already wounded?"

111

The outlaw's gaze drifted dreamily round to his wife. "Just—bringin' a surprise—back to her, was all . . . The wound didn't amount to much." He smiled and the girl smiled back. None of this made Grant Maxwell feel any better.

"It was a damned fool thing to do, boy," he exclaimed.

The outlaw looked back at the older man, still wearing his fading smile. "Yeah, sure was, wasn't it? I—didn't figure anyone'd be out—on a night like that. Lucky shot, Mister?"

Maxwell thought a moment before replying. "*Un*lucky shot, King."

They kept regarding one another, then the outlaw said, "You forgot to tell your rider to fetch back some whisky."

As Maxwell got heavily back upright he said, "Don't worry, he'll bring it anyway," then Maxwell turned and jerked his head at Verrill. The two of them were moving out of earshot when the girl called.

"Mister Maxwell . . . ?"

Grant and Verrill turned. She was holding a little nickel-plated revolver in her hand. She threw it over where it fell in the pine needles a yard from Maxwell's feet. Then she turned her back on the two men and leaned to finish washing her husband's gray face.

Maxwell handed the gun to Verrill, who silently pocketed it as he and Maxwell walked on another thirty or forty feet.

"That's it," said Maxwell, nodding his head towards

the pocket holding the little nickel-plated gun. "That's what I had to say to you, Verrill. If he had a cannon under the blankets, he couldn't use it. Not now; neither of them could get away."

"The girl could have."

Maxwell shook his head. "She wouldn't leave him. The only way she might try is if he dies."

Verrill's broad, low forehead puckered instantly. "You figure he will?"

Maxwell looked back where the outlaw was lying. "I think so, Verrill. I think he's just about out of blood. I hope to hell I'm wrong, but I'll tell you one thing you can depend upon; it's touch and go with him, and I wouldn't bet a red cent he'll ever leave here with his eyes open."

Verrill turned instinctively to look back, then in a lowered voice he said, "Maybe that's best, Mister Maxwell." His attitude seemed to change. Not softening; Norman Verrill was not a soft man, but he was rational and very practical, which he proved when next he spoke.

"They'll hang him sure as hell over in the Yellowstone country. There was a dead clerk after the bank robbery over there. Even if he wriggled out of that—which he never will do—Wyoming and Colorado got hold warrants out on him. He'll spend the rest of his lousy life in a penitentiary. In his boots, I think I'd prefer to just go to sleep and forget the whole damned thing."

Maxwell considered the detective a moment. "Are

you married, Mister Verrill?"

"Hell, no."

Maxwell's eyes puckered with a tough smile. "Then you don't know what you'd do in his boots, do you?"

Verrill did not pursue this. "She'll be wanted, too."

Maxwell's hard smile vanished. "For what?"

"Aiding and abetting; for conspiracy, and concealing knowledge of crimes. Hell, there are a dozen laws they can nail her on."

Maxwell said, "You know a lot of law, Mister Verrill. I'll tell you what I hope: that you never get married and have a daughter."

Verrill's antagonism returned. "Yeah? I'd raise mine a hell of a lot different than *that* little catamount was raised. I can tell you that for a plumb fact!"

Maxwell's hard smile returned. "No you can't. You can't tell me anything about raising a daughter, Mister Verrill. But maybe I can tell *you* something: no matter how hard you try, how much you want for them, and how good a job you do—someday a young, handsome, curly-headed young buck rides into the yard with the sun behind his back and a certain look in his eyes—and, Mister Verrill, believe me because I know—you die a thousand deaths because you know as sure as you know your own name that when he rides out, your daughter's going with him. . . . And only God knows whether he's an outlaw at heart, or maybe a successful mining engineer. By the time you find out, you've got a handful more of gray hairs."

Maxwell offered a genuine smile as he finished speaking. "You want to know why I didn't send word back to you last night or this morning that I knew where King was? Because that girl with him reminds me of my own daughter at her age. You want to arrest me, go right ahead."

They stood apart, looking at one another for a while, then Grant Maxwell stepped past the younger man and strolled back where Jane King was sitting, slumped and vanquished, looking at her first, and most magnificent, love. She did not seem aware of Grant Maxwell when he dropped to one knee on the far side of Al King's blanket-pallet. She did not seem aware of anything at all, except the one person on earth who was life and breath, sunshine and warmth, laughter and tenderness, love and meaning.

Maxwell, too, studied the wounded man. It crossed his mind that Al King was drifting back in time to his boyhood; he kept looking a little younger every time Maxwell saw him. Maybe it was because his color was steadily decreasing, that the hard lines around his eyes and lips were gradually smoothing out.

Chapter Thirteen

GUNS IN THE FOREST!

Verrill was probably by instinct a restless individual; perhaps that was what the Pinkerton Detective Agency had recognized as a valuable asset in him, and undoubtedly if he hadn't been restless he would not have remained on Al King's trail the way he had. But this same inability to be inactive for very long almost got him killed.

Grant Maxwell was squatting beside the wounded man. He and the girl were quietly talking. She seemed to have made a simple transfer of some inner need, from the wounded man, who hardly spoke any more at all, to big Grant Maxwell. She told him in a quiet monotone how, shortly after she and her husband arrived in Colorado with a wagon train they had traveled from Council Bluffs with, he got a job with a big cow outfit, but that he was dissatisfied. He had told her he wanted to be able to ride into a town and buy drinks for the boys in a saloon, and how he wanted to be able to stroll down a roadway with his wife, and when she saw a dress or a bonnet, or a pair of high-button shoes that she liked, he wanted to be able to waltz her into the store, throw down cash, and buy things for her.

"Maybe it was partly my fault, because I said those things would be nice. And the next thing I knew he and four other riders had formed a band. I didn't know it until the stage was raided south of Denver, and a big mercantile store was robbed, and he came for me one night, with his friends, and we rode hard until the next morning. . . . He showed me his share of the money . . . After that they got better; got cleverer, too. They would split up and raid in all directions; then rendezvous and pretend to be dirt farmers or squatters—like we did out there where I first saw you, Mister Maxwell—then we'd pull out at night and a couple of days later we'd be hundreds of miles away, in new country." She raised her gray eyes. "I told him we had enough. He said one more raid and we'd go back to Nebraska and buy a ranch and some fine cattle, and settle down to raise a fine family."

Grant Maxwell said nothing. These were the lyrics to a song he knew by heart.

". . . And this happened," she murmured, leaning slightly to look at her husband.

Maxwell looked at her. He did not have to look at her husband; everything that Al King had been, was now, and in Maxwell's private opinion, shortly would be, were in the man's face. Maxwell had seen all that many times before, too.

He said, "Do you have folks?"

She shook her head without looking back. "Not any more. They died of a sickness the winter after Al and I got married."

"Those other cowboys . . ."

She turned back, finally, and cast an indifferent glance over where Verrill was leaning the empty captured carbine against a tree. As Verrill turned to stroll closer to the edge of the trees where they fringed the little clearing which lay eastward, she said, "Just—other cowboys, Mister Maxwell. They couldn't see spending the rest of their lives working for twelve dollars a month, either."

Grant turned to see what she was watching. He, too, studied Norman Verrill's progress towards the fringe of trees. Verrill was probably going over across the park to the abandoned outlaw encampment to see what he could find among the abandoned things over there.

Then the gunshot came.

Maxwell was taken entirely by surprise. He saw Norman Verrill's legs go out from under him violently, saw the detective hit the ground hard, and saw a faint wisp of ancient dust fly from the bone-dry matting of needles. Then he was on his feet streaking for his six-gun. The girl was completely still; she did not seem to be breathing. The only one who did not even flicker an eyelid was her husband lying there upon his pallet.

Maxwell saw the gunman step away from the distant outlaw camp, a carbine held crossways, and take a couple of tentative steps forward.

There were two of them and the one slightly southward who came into Grant Maxwell's vision a moment later sang out to the rifleman, "You got him good. Now let's find the damned horse and get out of here."

Maxwell's mind raced. He could have shot the man with the carbine. The range would have been great, but he thought he could nail him.

But that did not grip his attention entirely, after the second one had called out. The outlaws, having seen just one man—Norman Verrill—had evidently decided to turn back and get Verrill's horse. They did not know Grant Maxwell was there at all, because they had never caught more than a fleeting glance, if that, of Maxwell and Farley, and it was more than just possible that they did not realize there was another man. If Jess had been there, there would have been two men.

But Jess was miles away, and the reason Grant Maxwell stood without moving, waiting and watching, was because if the entire band of those outlaws had come back for Verrill's horse Maxwell's life was not worth a plugged penny.

He turned slowly to look at the girl. She was watching him. She shook her head as though to say he did not have a chance, and he was tempted to agree with her. "Keep down," he told her, and started stealthily forward. When he came close to the tree where the detective had propped the carbine, he took it, and the empty six-gun, and hurled them as far up into the forest as he could. He did not really believe the girl would shoot him in the back, but he did not

119

have enough time to ask her. Also, thinking of his rangeboss, he knew what Jess's reaction to any such query would be.

The outlaw with the carbine was walking across the clearing. The other man, who had been southward just barely shadowed by the trees, was nowhere in sight. Maxwell guessed that this latter outlaw would be striding around the clearing heading for the place Al King and his wife were.

If the second man got up there, he would be behind Grant Maxwell. But Maxwell could not face in two directions at the same time, and because the man with the carbine was closest, and of proven deadliness, Maxwell angled slightly northward among the trees, hoping in this way to conceal himself from the hidden outlaw, and kept watching the unsuspecting man who was now walking boldly towards the lumpy sprawl that was Norman Verrill.

Maxwell had a moment to speculate on how much longer it would take the man making the circuit around through the trees to reach King's pallet, than it would take the oncoming outlaw who was making a direct, quick crossing of the park. If there could be perhaps a minute or two between them, Grant Maxwell thought he might survive, after all. One thing he was mortally certain of was that the oncoming man with the Winchester was as good as dead.

Verrill lay near the edge of the forest visible to Maxwell, who was to Verrill's left. He was also visible to the oncoming man with the carbine, but the outlaw seemed to share Maxwell's feeling that Verrill was dead; he had not moved so much as a hand, after the shooting.

Maxwell blended well with the gloom beneath the giant pine where he waited, half protected by rough tree-bark. The outlaw was almost to the trees over near Verrill when he stopped, or hesitated, looking all around before pressing onward, and *that* was when it dawned upon Maxwell that the other outlaws were not with these two. If they had been, by now there would have been some sign of them. That man with the carbine would not have acted so wary when he paused out there if another three or four men had been backing him up. Maxwell began to feel less fatalistic. He gauged the distance, let the outlaw cover another five yards, until the man was still in sunshine but only a few feet from forest-gloom, then Maxwell called him.

"Stop where you are! Drop that gun!"

The outlaw reacted like a striking snake. He dropped low and gave a mighty bound to reach the trees nearest him. He didn't have a chance. Grant Maxwell fired, thumbed back the hammer and fired again. The first shot missed by inches but the second slug caught the outlaw in mid-leap. He let go of the gun, threw out both hands and fell rolling. He fetched up limply against a fir tree, flopped back and turned flat his full length, face up.

Someone in the middle distance let off a shout; that had to be the other outlaw, startled by the pair of gunshots no doubt, and calling for reassurance. Maxwell could not give it, and the man lying flat out over against the fir tree was unable to give it. Maxwell's bullet had smashed his heart.

For five seconds there were only the bouncing echoes of Maxwell's two shots, then they faded in the distance and Maxwell eased around his tree looking for the second man. He wanted to go look at Verrill, but was afraid of moving for fear he would draw gunfire. He had no idea where that second man was.

A high flight of crows went past, overhead, in a typically ragged and garrulous formation, their complaining voices raised in discordant sound. That was all the movement or sound.

Maxwell finally moved, heading down towards Norman Verrill, but taking twice as much time as a man would normally have required to cover that little distance. He went from tree to tree, like an Indian, and waited behind each one until he could scan the onward forest for anything suspicious.

When he finally got close enough to Verrill, he waited a long time. The detective was lying exposed between two trees. Anyone approaching him, and halting out there, would be equally as vulnerable. He whirled at a slightly abrasive sound and saw the girl moving slowly, indifferently forward, her face composed, her body loose and slack. She went past Maxwell's tree as though she did not realize he was there; maybe she didn't, he hadn't moved since before he saw her coming.

She went over to Norman Verrill, knelt, and with strong, nut-brown arms rolled him gently on to his side. Maxwell saw the blood but the girl's back hid the wound. She was motionless for a moment, then she leaned and went to work fashioning a bandage out of Verrill's shirt-front.

Maxwell deduced from that that Verrill was not dead after all. The girl would not have bandaged a dead man.

Maxwell craned to his left, back in the direction of the wounded man's pallet. Unless that other outlaw had been scared off, had turned back to flee, he would probably home-in on that place. Maxwell moved soundlessly back deeper into the forest, keeping his attention in the three most threatening directions.

He eventually got back where he could see the wounded man lying still as stone upon his old blankets. If that other outlaw fled, it would suit Grant Maxwell very well. But until he knew without any question that the man *had* fled, he was living on borrowed time.

Finally, after what seemed like an eternity of waiting, Maxwell started a tree-to-tree stalk up and far around the wounded man's pallet, seeking a way to scout up the area where the other outlaw had to be— unless he had gone back.

Little warning sounds were strong in the back of his mind. There was no way to protect his back; if he went too far and the outlaw appeared behind him, Maxwell would probably never hear the gunshot.

He was thirsty and the heat seemed to have increased five-fold. Also, it was close and confining and stifling in the scented forest. Maxwell halted longest beside a lightning-struck huge old fir tree. There he waited for his spirit to shrug off the premonitions and tensions.

He estimated that since shooting the first outlaw, perhaps a half-hour had elapsed. The deeper he went into the area where that other man had been, without seeing or hearing anything, the more certain he became that the second renegade had turned back at the sound of gunshots and was now perhaps out where his horse was, willing to save his own life by abandoning his partner.

Finally, Maxwell spent another half-hour searching, and located some tracks showing where a man had come forward, then had turned back. The last set showed deep, wide imprints; the outlaw had been running.

Maxwell paused to push sweat off his face with a sleeve, then, with less caution, tracked down the second set of tracks. He found where a horse had been tethered, where someone had sprang up astride the horse and had whirled away, riding swiftly in an easterly direction along through the lowest fringe of trees.

Satisfied, finally, he turned back towards Al King's pallet. The girl was there, washing her hands from a canteen. She looked up without speaking, then looked down and finished her washing. Finally, she stood up, offered Maxwell the canteen, and padded silently over to kneel in her customary place beside her husband.

Chapter Fourteen

THE WAYS MEN DIE

Grant Maxwell went out where Norman Verrill lay and helped the detective sit up with his thick shoulders against a tree. Verrill's wound was not where Maxwell had thought—through the body. Maxwell had made that snap judgment from the way he had seen Verrill go down. The carbine bullet had struck alongside Verrill's head on an upward-angling course, something that mystified Maxwell since both Verrill and the outlaw had been standing up, facing towards one another. Then Maxwell saw the raw gouge upon a close-by tree and understood that the bullet had struck there first, and had been deflected upwards. So, it had not been the direct shot that it had appeared to be.

Verrill was groggy and weak as a kitten. He had not actually shed much blood, although his hair under the girl's improvised bandage, as well as the cloth, were soggy and matted, but he had most certainly come within a hair's breadth of getting a concussion; in relation to a Winchester's steel-jacketed bullet, a man's skull, no matter how thick it might be, was no more than an eggshell.

Grant explained what had happened. Verrill looked around from copiously watering eyes, and cursed unsteadily because of his headache. Then he saw the dead outlaw, flat out near a big tree, and his complaining stopped.

"Is that the one who shot me?" he asked, and although Maxwell nodded his head without speaking, something Verrill probably did not see because he was staring at the dead man, the detective said, "Were there only the pair of them? You sure nailed him plumb center, didn't you?"

Maxwell answered neither question. He stood up and leaned upon a tree and looked back where the pallet was. When Verrill finally said, "I'm dry enough to drink a lake dry," Maxwell extended a rough hand and hauled the injured man to his feet. Then, finally, he spoke.

"The girl patched you up. I didn't dare go out there. Come along, there's water at the place where the Kings are."

Verrill was a large, heavy man. Maxwell was no midget, but he had all he could do, supporting the detective back. When he finally eased the younger man down and reached for the canteen, the detective looked over where the girl was sitting looking steadily at her husband, and said, "I appreciate what you did."

The girl might as well have been deaf. She looked up at Grant Maxwell and softly said, "He's dead."

Grant handed over the canteen, then twisted to drop

126

to one knee opposite the girl. She was correct; her husband was dead.

Maxwell had been in this situation before, too, but each passing is different to some degree, and although he knew all the words normally used, when he wanted to fit them together into a fresh meaning for this particular situation, he could not do it because none of them sounded really appropriate.

He leaned closer and studied the waxen face. As he did this the girl said, "Some time back. Right after the shooting started, he called my name—and just—died."

Maxwell looked at the girl. That had been before she had risked her life walking down there to tend Verrill. He remembered, now, how limp she had looked, how dull and apathetic in the face she had been. Still, she had gone over to see if she could help Verrill.

Maxwell rocked back and let out a big breath in silence. A lot of thoughts ran through his mind; the wages of sin is death, I shall repay, saith the Lord, and another thought that had to do with something Maxwell believed very firmly in because he had seen it work time and time again: the law of retribution.

Jane King reminded Maxwell of Indian squaws he had seen sitting like that, on their haunches, rocking very gently, very slightly, unable to shed a single tear beside the bier of their husbands, dying an inch at a time, inside.

He told himself she was young, that she would recover in time. It was a consoling variety of thought.

But of the actual mechanics of living, of how *they* would treat her, he had no idea.

Verrill lit a cigarette, something Maxwell could not recall ever having seen the man do before. Not that it mattered in the slightest.

Maxwell got to his feet again and walked down through the trees until he could see across the park. Then he went farther down, southward, which was in the approximate direction he had previously stalked that fleeing outlaw. Down there, he squatted for a long time watching the open, gold-lighted, easterly range for some sign of riders, of Jess Farley returning with the GM range crew.

All he saw was a little band of aimlessly wandering sleek cattle, probably Frazier's critters since they were on his range, so he got upright and walked back again.

The girl was nowhere in sight, but Verrill was standing, beginning to look better and to act stronger. When the detective saw Maxwell's glance around, he said, "I let her go. What the hell . . ." Verrill looked meaningfully at the dead man, shrugged and looked back at Maxwell. "She's in pretty bad shape."

Grant Maxwell would not have argued that point, but the girl had had only one thing to hold her to this place, and now that reason no longer existed except as a corpse.

But Maxwell said nothing; if the girl escaped, so much the better, although he had very strong doubts about her ability to survive alone and unarmed in the mountains.

Verrill had different thoughts. "I went back and searched that dead one. His name was on a letter: Jeff Dowling."

Maxwell was unimpressed. He stooped and pulled a blanket up over Al King's composed, bloodless face.

"What's bothering me is all that money," said Verrill. "I wish you'd sent your rangeboss back last night instead of this morning. By now we'd be on the trail."

The girl materialized soundlessly. Maxwell saw movement among the trees and faced it. She walked ahead looking fresher, as though she had recently scrubbed her face at the creek. She saw that someone had pulled the blanket over her husband's face and although she resumed a sitting position, like a vigil, beside the body, she did not turn back the blanket.

Maxwell went over and leaned against a tree near her. "There is no easy way to come to grips with it," he told her. "I know. I was married a long time; the parting was hard."

The girl looked upwards, face impassive.

He smiled a little down at her. "We'll take him back and see that he gets a decent send-off."

She said, "Where? In that ugly little town?"

"No. At my ranch. We have our own cemetery shaded by some tamarack trees. There's an iron railing around it to keep critters out. . . . My wife's buried there."

The gray eyes clung to Maxwell. "Why, Mister Maxwell . . . ?"

"Well, I'm not his judge, Jane, and neither are you

or Mister Verrill. And now that's all finished with, for him. So give me one reason why not?"

"Your wife probably would not have approved."

Maxwell's smile got stronger. "You didn't know my wife, Jane. She'd approve. In fact, if she was standing here right now, she'd insist."

Verrill listened a little, then went meandering away, slowly, because he had a headache and his limbs were still shaky, but his was a restless personality. The girl watched, and eventually said, "I'll have to go back with him, won't I?"

Maxwell declined to commit himself. "That's between you and him." He switched the subject. "Jane, how much money do those outlaws have with them?"

She made a bitter grimace. "All of it. My husband told them that part of it belonged to him, and for them to give it to me. They didn't. I never expected them to. The actual amount? I don't know, Mister Maxwell, but I think they must have about eighteen or twenty thousand dollars."

That was an immense fortune. Even split four or five ways, it was an awful lot of money.

Maxwell asked another question. "How come them to light out in this direction; do they know the mountains?"

Jane King nodded. "That was part of their strategy; Al believed in it too. Wherever we stopped, the men would spend about a week riding everywhere. They know these mountains. They also knew the prairie

130

around Laramie, and over as far as Cheyenne." Her gray eyes lingered on his face. "If you're asking because you plan to run them down—I doubt that you'll be able to do it."

Maxwell was confident. "We'll run them down. As long as they keep traveling west, all they are going to do is wear out their horses. There are no ranches or cow camps in that direction for about a hundred miles. Just mountains beyond mountains."

She was stubborn. "They know about that. Last night they talked about it. They also know that if they cut northward they'll find fresh animals and some cow outfits."

That, of course, was true. Grant Maxwell looked up, trying to gauge the time of day by the sun, but those stiff-topped trees cut out all direct sight of the sun. Still, he guessed it had to be about noon. He also guessed that Jess should be arriving in another hour, or hour and a half. Men on horseback could cover a lot of distance when there was nothing to hold them back, and when they had an adequate incentive to move fast.

The girl said, "What will you do with me, when the others arrive?"

"Send you back—with him—in the wagon, I reckon. You can't go with us after the men, and I don't know what else to do with you." Maxwell removed his hat and wiped off perspiration, pulled the hat back down and said, "Maybe the detective will ride back, too."

From back in the forest-gloom a voice said, "No, thanks. I'll go along with the rest of you." Verrill had their two horses. He led them on up and handed Maxwell his reins. "I've had worse hurts than this just from breaking up saloon brawls. I'm all right."

Maxwell could have argued that point. It was one thing to stop a saloon fight, then sit down and catch one's breath, and something altogether different to ride, perhaps for days, on half rations or no rations, through rough and rugged mountainous country, chasing armed outlaws. But if Verrill wanted to try it, Maxwell did not particularly care one way or the other. He turned to tie his horse and Verrill said, "They are coming. I made them out about two miles back. It looks like your whole crew, Mister Maxwell. I think I counted about six men. Is that right?"

It was right, but all the cowman said was, "Better water these horses, then, if we're going to be on the trail directly," and turned his back on Verrill to take his mount to the creek.

Verrill followed along. When they were standing, waiting for the horses to finish drinking, Verrill said in a soft voice that the girl should be tied on the ride back.

Maxwell looked around. "Not while I'm in charge," he said, and Verrill's bloodshot eyes narrowed.

"Who said you were in charge?"

Maxwell's answer was cold. "You saw six of my men. Now who the hell would you figure would be in charge?"

They finished watering the horses and went back. The girl was busy wrapping her husband's body by rolling it in the old, soiled blankets. She needed something to do. It pained Grant Maxwell to watch.

He heard a whoop from the southeast, and moments later Jess rode in, his carbine in one hand. Jess had seen the dead outlaw back near the fringe of forest. As he got down and glanced over where the girl was finishing her work, Jess raised dark, quizzical eyes to his employer.

"A couple of them came back to get Verrill's horse. I shot that one who passed, the other one ran for it."

Farley accepted this and pointed. "Him?"

Verrill said, "Dead. Died about the time the outlaws struck." Verrill raised a hand to his bandaged head. "A graze, it's nothing."

Jess sighed, looked over his shoulder where the other GM horsemen were beginning to appear, and said, "We brought back a bottle of rotgut, Boss, and a team for the wagon." He turned back and looked gravely past Maxwell where Jane King was sitting back on her haunches again, staring at the neatly rolled body of her husband. "What about her?"

"One of you goes back," explained Maxwell. "The girl goes back too. Verrill ought to, but he won't, so he can ride with us."

Jess nodded. "I reckon he won't need the rotgut, then. Well, we got about six hours of daylight left. Maybe we'd better get to moving."

Verrill said, "You tell your man, the one who takes

the corpse back, and the girl, to be damned careful. If she can she'll grab his gun."

Farley's dark gaze swept over Verrill as he turned, without commenting, and went back where the riders were standing in tree-shade looking down at the dead outlaw.

Chapter Fifteen

THE OUTLAWS' TRAIL

They carried the blanket-wrapped body back to the wagon, got the rig turned around and hitched to the team from the ranch, then, with one of the riders on the wagon-seat, his saddle animal tied to the tailgate, there were still five GM riders beside their horses, plus the detective, and plus Grant Maxwell. He gave the girl a hand up over the rear hub and into the wagon, then he said, "When you reach the ranch, go on up where you'll see my cemetery and pick your place for him. And wait." He stopped speaking. He was supposed to say something else, but instead he turned and toed into the stirrup and rose up over leather.

Verrill also got astride. He probably intended to speak to the girl, perhaps to warn her or at least offer an official admonition, but Grant Maxwell happened to turn his horse in such a way that it blocked Verrill, then Jess Farley said, "Let's get to moving," and they all headed back down across the little empty park on a southerly course, heading for the tracks the escaping outlaws had made. Verrill did not get to speak to the girl after all, but a mile or so onward, when they were heading out on to the range to the west, Grant Maxwell rode up and said, "I think she'll be there when we get back."

Verrill had already made his judgment about that. "If she isn't, I can find her easy enough, but even if I didn't ever see her again, she's not important in relation to what's up ahead."

Maxwell thought that was a fair way to look at it. If Verrill had gone back with the girl, of course, he would have had one living prisoner and one dead prisoner, and maybe, if the Maxwell riders were lucky, they might have brought him back another outlaw or so; this was probably all the Pinkerton Detective Agency expected of Verrill. But a conscientious man in Verrill's boots would hope to do better, and hope to net the entire band of outlaws.

Maxwell hoped Verrill's wound would not slow them. He did not expect to stop, now that he was on the outlaws' trail, whether Verrill's headache got worse or not. Every man had his personal motives, and Maxwell's were to overtake the outlaws and fetch them back, one way or another, then get on with his everyday way of living; he had no intention at all of prolonging this. It had already gone on long enough.

Jess Farley was far out front when the sign cut northward back into the trees a mile and a half from where the outlaws had halted a lifetime ago to watch the approach of Norman Verrill. Jess and one of the other riders, another older man, sat together a moment before riding up into the forest, talking, then the other cowboy pushed off first and was lost to sight within moments. Jess followed, and behind him the others walked their horses back into the shade again.

There were canteens along, although no one really expected to be unable to locate creeks in the mountains, and they all had food in their saddlebags. All, that is, except Maxwell and Verrill, but there was enough for them, too. There was also enough ammunition. When Jess had got to the ranch and had shouted up the riders, he had stressed ammunition and food.

The rider Farley had sent ahead was a good tracker. Later, Jess told Grant Maxwell this particular cowboy, called Chet, was the best tracker of them all, which was making quite an admission since Jess Farley was a good man at reading sign.

Farley rode a few miles alongside his employer. They conversed a little, but not a lot. Both were tough, capable men, but both had been pushing themselves hard for more than twenty-four hours, and no matter how hard a man's resolve might be, his body was still susceptible to fatigue. Maxwell felt more sleepy than actually tired. When he mentioned this Jess offered the bottle of whisky, but Maxwell declined with a grin; whisky made him drowsy even when he was rested, he said.

The trail was not difficult to follow. Once the cowboy who was scouting on ahead sat and waited, and when the others came up he pointed to a notch against the horizon. "They're heading up there, following an old game trail," he reported. "They may veer off, but from the lie of the country I'd guess they won't. I'd also guess they know this trail." The cowboy sat a moment, ranging his narrowed gaze up towards the notch, then he said, "If I was in their boots, I'd get high enough before the sun goes down, to rest m' horse, and I'd look back down here, figurin' that if I was being followed whoever was behind me would have to cross one of the little parks on this trail sooner or later, and I'd see 'em." The cowboy looked from Jess to Grant Maxwell, and smiled. "And if I was one of the followers, I'd skirt out and around them little parks."

Grant said, "Go ahead, skirt around them," and as the rider turned and rode onward Grant leaned towards Jess with his private idea about being seen from higher up the mountain slope. "If those outlaws aren't any farther along than three, four miles on up towards that pass, Jess, I'll be surprised. They've had the whole damned day to get through the notch and down the far side."

It was something to think about, but discussing it wouldn't change anything, one way or the other, so

Jess merely nodded and urged his horse out again, with the others following.

The trail did, indeed, cross a number of parks; after all, it *was* a game trail, and while it was true that most big game in the mountains of Wyoming were foragers rather than grazing animals, it was also true that a browsing animal also ate grass, and, even more important, the open glens usually had water in them. Once, they crossed a stretch of trail where a bear had passed through only a short while earlier. Aside from his sign, they noticed that the drowsy horses suddenly grew alert and wary, which meant the scent was still in the air. Otherwise, though, they encountered nothing until they were angling along the far uphill slope, when they interrupted a family of elk in an aspen grove, and that brought the horses up in the bit again. But the elk, startled far more than the horsemen, left the area with a great snorting and crashing sound as they charged down the hill towards the lower country.

The sun was still up there, and daylight lingered, but there were shadows on the east side of trees and, when they got higher, on the east side of great stone outcroppings as well, which meant that day would not last much longer. Of course, it was summer now, and there would be light for a couple of hours even after the sun set.

What Grant Maxwell was counting upon was getting through the pass up ahead before daylight ended. On the far side was a downhill ride through more forest for perhaps six miles, but beyond that was another span of the Laramie Plains which ran north-ward and westward for many miles, and which of course also ran eastward back in the direction of the towns of Laramie and Cheyénne. It was cow country, and not altogether different from the range around Jelm, except that it had no town.

Maxwell knew that country. As a young man he had even considered staking his claim out there. The reason that he'd selected the area around Jelm instead was because up ahead there was no major thorough-fare. There were roads and trails, but they were used by cowmen, not by the stagelines, and that put a man pretty much out of touch with the world. At least, that was how it had been thirty years ago when Grant Maxwell had been looking the country over for a place to put down roots. Of course, since then, there had been changes. Even so, he had never regretted his choice. He had ridden over here several times, over the past fifteen or twenty years, to drive home way-ward GM critters, usually steers—the genuine adven-turers of the cow country—and progress had shown itself to be very reluctant about settling on the far western end of the Laramie Plains.

By the time Jess met Chet atop the pass, with the others coming ploddingly up behind, Maxwell had noticed that the Pinkerton detective was beginning to look bad. He rode like a sack of meal and his face was pale and sweat-shiny. Maxwell said nothing; he got up where his two men waited, and motioned for them to keep going. Later, when Jess dropped back to ride stirrup with Maxwell, the rancher said, "We're going to have to call a halt by the time we get through the forest, yonder, or that detective's going to cave-in on us."

Jess looked back, looked forward, and sighed. "I had my doubts when we struck out," he muttered. "The damned fool should have gone back with the wagon." Then Jess looked at Maxwell and asked a question. "You figure to let him stop us?"

Maxwell shook his head.

Ordinarily they would have stopped to rest the stock just below the summit, one side or the other—not *at* the summit, particularly if the horses were hot from climbing and there was wind up there; that was the best way in the world to chest-founder horses—but Grant Maxwell made the decision and they went down the far side with barely more than a pause. It was not particularly hard on the horses, they were going *down*hill, finally, and Maxwell had his doubts about ever getting Norman Verrill under way again if they let him sit and stock-up.

The others understood. Verrill's deteriorating condition was plain enough, but no one spoke aloud concerning it, and among the cowboys farther back it was decided to take turns riding with the detective to talk to him, to keep him alert and if possible to cheer him up.

Jess went on ahead to find the tracker, and Grant Maxwell brought up the rest of the horsemen. When he next saw Jess, the rangeboss was on foot beside his horse poking in a little churned-earth area where evidently someone—the outlaws undoubtedly—had nooned. Jess turned up several tins, and a smashed pony of whisky, which aroused only mild interest. Grant Maxwell found a bent horseshoe draped across a low limb where a young fir tree stood, and *that* even got a smile from Norman Verrill. If one horse had shed a worn-out shoe, then others might do the same, but whether they did or not, one thing was sure; that three-footed horse was going to wear his hoof down fast from here on, in the shale country, and that was a good sign for the trackers. One of the GM cowboys facetiously turned the worn-out shoe upright and pegged it to the tree where it had been found as a good-luck omen. The men laughed. Even Verrill grinned. Then they went on again.

Someone handed Verrill a sardine tin. He ate the contents as he allowed his horse to follow Maxwell's mount down the trail. Once, when Grant looked back and saw the detective wiping greasy fingers on his trousers, Verrill shrugged and said, "It isn't the first suit of clothes I've ruint doing things like this. It's the Agency's idea that all operatives should dress well and look decent, not mine."

The sun left, finally. Maxwell told Jess to get up ahead and tell Chet to shag along a little faster, if possible, so they wouldn't be caught in the forest when darkness arrived.

After Jess departed Maxwell tried to evolve a schedule, but of course that was impossible; for one thing the tracks they were following did not always go straight down the slope; for another thing, unless a man knew exactly how far out the trees went upon the plain in this particular area, he wouldn't have much of an idea how far he had yet to ride through them.

Still, Grant thought they could get clear of the forest, with a little luck, before nightfall. Jess came along, midway down, to say that Chet had an idea the outlaws were heading like an arrow for the prairie yonder, and that was a good bit of news.

Jess also said, as he and Grant rode together between the trees, that for horses carrying double, the mounts being used by the outlaws were either unusually tough and durable, or else they had to be on the verge of collapse.

Maxwell had wondered about that earlier, as they were beginning the ascent. His own mount was sweating hard by the time they reached the summit; he speculated about the condition of the horses up ahead carrying twice the load.

Chet appeared, eventually, as the downhill cavalcade came through a burnt-out clearing. He pointed over where someone had flung a bedroll and a pair of saddlebags. No one commented, but the evidence was clear that at least *one* horse was giving out.

They came to the last of the trees, finally, and good fortune was on their side; where they sat a moment in the final fringe of forest, the terrain sucked back forming a kind of inland clearing with sweeping stands of forest on both sides. Ahead was open country. Daylight was better, but it was not going to last much longer, even out there.

Maxwell wanted to rest the horses, but he gestured for Chet to pick up the trail out upon the plain and keep going, which is what they did, leaving the forest and the mountain slope behind them.

Chapter Sixteen

ON THROUGH THE NIGHT

Although this was turn-out time of year, had been in fact for about six weeks, the Maxwell posse did not see any cattle. Of course, there were a dozen reasonable explanations for this; cattle did not go near forests unless the heat or something else drove them to do so, and not entirely because the pickings were slim where resin soured the ground, but also because forests were where catamounts and bears lay in wait for weak cows and little calves.

But when they were more than a mile out upon the plain and still saw no critters, Grant Maxwell wondered a little. On his range it was usually possible to see cattle when a man had covered a mile or so of open country, in almost any direction.

The tracks were still heading northward. Also, now that they were out of the forest, they were much easier to follow. As Jess said, if they had a full moon they wouldn't have to halt at all.

But they did not have a full moon, the horses were dragging, and Norman Verrill was clutching his saddlehorn to keep from reeling in the saddle.

Maxwell called a halt near a creek lined with willows. The men got down stiffly, off-saddled, went to the creek to wash the backs of their horses, and afterwards to sit upon the motionless ground, quite a contrast to what else they had been sitting on since mid-afternoon without respite. Some smoked, some ate, and some, like Verrill, just flopped back flat out and rested.

Chet stood with Grant Maxwell and Jess Farley. The sign, he thought, was holding to an arrow-straight course directly across the plain towards the far-away mountains. "But they ain't going to be very far out," he said. "Those horse-tracks were scuffing dirt pretty bad. They got to rest them animals soon or they're going to end up on foot. Ain't no horse ever been borned can keep this up, carrying double. My guess is that we're maybe no more'n two miles, at the most three miles, behind them boys."

Jess nodded without commenting, and when Chet walked over to join the other resting men at the creek, Jess said, "I'll go scout ahead a ways on foot. Be better'n ridin' up on 'em in the dark and have the horses whinny and give us away."

Grant was willing. After Jess walked away Maxwell also went over to the creek. He had been traveling on stamina and little else for a number of hours; he knew what would happen the moment he sat down and relaxed, and it *did* happen. He stretched out and was asleep within moments. Nearby, the younger cowboys were lounging, physically tired but not sleepy, so they could loll and smoke, and take an occasional pull from the bottle of whisky, and be ready to ride again after the horses were rested.

Verrill also slept, and he snored, something men who lived close together in bunkhouses did not approve of but of which they said nothing tonight. If they had been in the bunkhouse they'd have broken Verrill of that with an occasional bucket of water, but this was different.

The rider who had done the tracking said he was sure they'd overtake the outlaws before noon tomorrow, even if they didn't hit the trail again until an hour or two before dawn. His reason was exactly as he had given it to Maxwell and Farley.

"Them horses are just about done for. Even a few hours of rest ain't going to make that much differ-ence."

One of the younger men, speaking the drawl of Texas, said, "If those old boys got a lick o' sense they'll peel off up ahead somewhere and go find themselves a corral full of fresh horses."

Someone snorted in the gloom. "Where? I never seen such a dad-blasted big, flat chunk of nowhere before in all my life. Don't even have cattle running up in here. Now where them boys goin' to find a corral?"

Chet knew. "East of here a few miles is a communal workin' ground, where these cowmen up in here make their midsummer and autumn gather. They'll be horses over there as sure as I'm a foot tall."

Another rider, lying back, arms under his head, looking straight up, said, "East of here there's plenty of places. The closer a feller'd get to Laramie the better pickings he'd have."

Someone asked what was westward and Chet removed his hat to vigorously scratch his thatch as he answered. "Maybe eight, ten miles of plain, then more lousy mountains. No ranches, if that's what you're gettin' at, but there's a couple of gathering grounds—only they aren't used this early in the year. No—those boys got to go east, if they figure to get fresh horses. And by gawd, was I in their boots, I wouldn't mess around going north another step. Whether they know it or not, there's not a damned thing but miles of plain, then more mountains in that direction, all the way up to the Montana border."

Someone coughed and spat, then lay back with a big groan in the soft-warm night and said, "You know what I think? Any man who forks a horse for a living is a damned imbecile. A plain, out-and-out simple-minded imbecile."

The men chuckled. Another rider had a response. "It's awful onhandy herding cattle on foot, Tad."

The man who had groaned answered back. "All right. Now tell me something: what does it do to a man's brains, spending all his life riding a horse behind cattle and lookin' at the rear-end of cows and bulls and steers? I'll *tell* you what it does: directly you get to thinkin' with the wrong end of your anatomy. Like sitting on a saddle all the time. That's using the wrong end to make your living with, isn't it?"

The men were amused, but the older riders like Chet smoked in quiet thought, because there came a time in every rangeman's life when he clearly saw himself five years, ten years hence, and nothing was really changed but *him*. He was older, a little slower, a lot stiffer on cold mornings and a lot more sluggish on hot summertime days.

It was the bald truth; when a man made his living across leather he was for a fact using the wrong end of his carcass to make his living.

But there was more to it than that: when the only tools a man was handy with consisted of saddle-leather, bridleleather, ropes and shoeing implements, corrals and chutes, what chance did he have at surviving in any other environment?

Chet killed his smoke, lay back, tipped down his hat and caught forty winks. Whatever the future held for a man, it held for him, and that was all there was to it.

Jess returned late. None of the men heard him coming, but the horses did. They were tanked up on water and bellyful of grass, so they did not snort nor offer to skitter away, all shy and leary at the rank scent of man-sweat, but they stared hard as he emerged out of the darkness heading for the camp, where he shook Chet and Grant Maxwell awake.

"Found 'em," he told those two, after they had sat up and rubbed their eyes awake. "About three miles northeast, like maybe they are figuring on skirting up around Laramie—or something, anyway."

Chet muttered his judgment. "Not the town; they're lookin' for a cow-camp or a ranch-corral. The nearest one's about six miles from here."

Jess punched holes in a tin of pork and beans and tipped back his head to eat. With his mouth full he said, "I think there are only three of them left. Evidently that feller you scairt off, Boss, didn't head back to join his friends." Jess swallowed with an effort, then said, "I got to thinkin' on the hike back that this feller must figure his friends can't make it. Otherwise, why would he abandon his share of that loot?"

It was good reasoning, but Grant Maxwell was not interested in why one of the outlaws had abandoned his friends; he was interested in catching the three outlaws who were still on the run, and it crossed his mind that unless he and his men were able to do this before the outlaws found a remuda of fresh horses, there was an excellent chance that they would *never* catch them, because their own mounts were not fresh either, rest notwithstanding.

Grant said, "Let's move out," and shoved up to his feet. He felt dull and had cobwebs inside his head, but that would pass. He hadn't had much sleep, but he'd had more than he had expected to get.

Chet routed out the other men. Everyone rigged out and got ready to ride. It was past midnight, that much

148

Grant guessed from the position of the sickle-moon, but it could have been as late as one or two in the morning, for all he actually knew, when they left the willows riding behind Jess Farley, who did not take the trail left by the outlaws, but who cut diagonally across the empty land, riding northeasterly.

This would save them a little time and perhaps a mile or two. As Jess told Grant when they were riding together, "We been damned lucky. By all rights those fellers, with a six-hour lead, ought to be so far ahead come dawn we wouldn't even be able to see their dust. I reckon we'll catch up to them this morning."

That set Grant to thinking. In open country like the Laramie Plains, there was no way to ambush anyone. Nor was there any way to approach without being seen. Those outlaws would not have to know who the men arriving from the direction of the southward mountains were, to realize that they had come in pursuit—and that meant a battle.

Unless, of course, the outlaws found fresh horses first, in which case there would still be a fight, but a running one, and with the odds favoring the outlaws.

The Indians had lost this same country because the same vulnerability had existed for them as now existed for Maxwell's men: there was no cover, no way to use tactics; if one party was fresh-mounted, they won. That was all there was to it. Winning for both the Indians and the outlaws meant escaping unhurt.

Maxwell turned to Jess and said, "We're not going

to catch them this morning, Jess, if they get fresh horses under them. We may get a sighting, but that's about all we'll get."

Farley made a smoke in silence, lit it and rode along without disputing this. He eventually stood in the stirrups because they were approaching the place where he expected to intersect that eastward trail of the fleeing men. What Jess could only guess about was how far the outlaws might be on ahead. If they were making better time on their rested animals than they had made the day before, they should be at least two miles ahead. If not, the Maxwell party could blunder right up on to them, and Jess didn't want anything like that to happen.

He put out his smoke when it was still only half-used, then he concentrated on watching his horse's head. The animals would detect new scents long before their riders could pick up sound or see movement in the watery gloom.

It was cold. The men had put on their jumpers, all but Verrill who had none, but he had his suit coat. It was not designed to actually provide much warmth, but the night wasn't all that cold either. The moon was far down, the stars were weakening, and there came a creeping, false kind of flat lightness to the whole sky. False dawn usually presaged real dawn by more than an hour, and it would eventually fade out, too.

Chet spurred up beside Jess to converse briefly, then he dropped back to ride with the other men who were clustering behind Maxwell a few yards.

Jess took his time with his thoughts, then eventually he edged closer to Maxwell and said, "Chet worked up here last summer. He says there's a big outfit southeast, and they got a working ground about another mile and a half on ahead."

Maxwell nodded his head. He knew the outfit, knew its owner, and he also knew where that holding-ground was. What he doubted was that there would be a crew camped up there. All the early marking and branding had been done a month and more back. There could be reasons for a fresh gather, but on his own range he only worked the herds twice a year, in the spring and in the autumn. He thought most cow outfits operated the same way, and in this country he *knew* most of them did because he was familiar with almost all the original owners and settlers.

But it was that off-chance that decided him to be safe. "If they are up ahead, Jess, they are going to hear us pretty soon now, or some damn-fool horse will nicker. I don't like the idea of splitting up, but I reckon I'd better take three men and head out and around, to the northeast, just in case you and the other fellers spook those men—*if* they are up there—and the outlaws make a break for it."

Farley nodded solemnly. "It'll be even odds now," he said. "That's better'n it was yesterday." Farley smiled in the watery paleness, and Grant reined sideways to call the men to him. He purposely did not call Verrill. As he led the way out and around at an easy lope, Verrill started to call out. Jess snarled him into immediate silence.

"You damned fool, they can hear a yell two miles on a night like this!"

Jess meant it. He was angered and Norman Verrill could see that. He did not complete his call.

Chapter Seventeen

OUT-SMARTED!

It hit Maxwell, finally, why he had not seen any cattle. There *was* a round-up taking place. The way he knew this was so, was when a little pre-dawn breeze brisked up and carried the strong scent out to him, while he and his men were loping northward, up and around the gathering-ground.

If there was a round-up in progress, then of course there was a remuda of saddle stock down there, too. He swore to himself, and began to hope against hope that the outlaws would do something accidentally that would rouse the camp. But that was not very likely. Those outlaws knew, better even than Maxwell knew, that this was their last best chance; they would not do anything to ruin it.

One of the cowboys said, "Mister Maxwell, you catch the smell of a big herd?"

Grant answered that he had detected the scent back

a ways. "That means a gather," he added, "and it also means a camp down there with a remuda."

The cowboy squinted skyward, then said, "If them outlaws is going to catch fresh mounts, they'd better be gettin' at it."

This was also true; the false dawn was receding, the night was settling down in full darkness again, and shortly now true dawn would come. The outlaws would be cutting it very fine. They had an interval of not more than perhaps a half-hour to find the remuda and switch their rigs on to fresh horses, but it wasn't the return of soft gloom that Grant Maxwell was considering; it was the fact that cow-camp crews traditionally rolled out very early, and that fact made it even more hazardous for the outlaws.

Grant halted his riders north of the gathering-ground, where the scent was strongest, and listened. The cattle would be stirring shortly now, heaving up out of their beds to go ambling off to graze, but what Maxwell, the lifelong cowman, was trying to detect, was the lowing of alarm from cattle roused out of their sleep by man-scent. He had to have some idea from which direction the outlaws were trying to reach the remuda.

He considered sending a man in closer to find the horse-herd, but in the end he decided to go himself, with his men, for while there was undeniable danger of being mistaken for horse thieves by the rangeriders, and there was an even greater danger of being fired upon by the outlaws, to whom *any* rider was an enemy now, if he could at least prevent the outlaws from getting freshly mounted, he would have won.

Someone stirred life into some coals by pitching on a handful of leaves and twigs. That would be the cook, who had to stir at least a half-hour before the camp came to life. Maxwell put that little guttering fire on his left and rode down straight southward where the smell kept getting stronger. The horse-herd would be inside a rope corral, and from long experience Maxwell knew about where it would be, in relation to the camp proper.

He was grateful for one thing; in cow camps there were rarely ever dogs, which was exactly the opposite of sheep camps, but then there were only a very few sheep camps on the Laramie Plains—yet.

A dog would have picked up the scent of approaching strangers and would have raised Cain. The only notice Maxwell's men got was from a jenny mule, probably one of a team used to haul the cook's wagon. She made her see-sawing, unmelodious call looking up in the direction of Maxwell's men.

Then Maxwell heard the sound he had been wondering about. When cattle were spooked out of their beds on the range they sprang up and hit the ground hard with their hooves. A horse did the same thing, but a horse also snorted or whistled, then ran. Cattle as often as not made no sound, unless it was a bravo bull or an anxious old fighting cow with a baby calf, but when a number of cattle sprang up suddenly in fright and stamped, the sound carried.

Maxwell heard it, and held up a hand as his riders turned, facing the southwest. When the sound was repeated Maxwell flipped the tie-down off his holstered gun and booted his horse over into a little tight lope. If his guess was correct, he could intercept the outlaws before they reached the camp. He motioned for the men to fan out a little.

Finally, he saw two horsemen ambling up through the gloom. There should have been three. Maxwell drew his six-gun, cocked it, and strained around trying to find the third man. He did not find him, but the other two had stopped in their tracks. Maxwell aimed at them and rode right on up. His men converged from three sides. The horsemen looked around, saw themselves being surrounded, and sat there.

When Maxwell got closer one of the riders spoke out in a plaintive tone of voice, saying, "Hey; what in hell you boys think you're doing?"

Maxwell looked from the men to their horses. Those animals were not tucked up at all. It dawned on Maxwell what he had done just as that same complaining man said, "Hey; ain't you Grant Maxwell from down around Jelm?"

Those two were nighthawks; cowboys who took turns riding round a big gather during the night to keep anything from spooking the animals, and to also keep any cutbacks from sneaking away from the gather in the darkness.

Maxwell said, "Where is the remuda?"

One of the astonished horsemen pointed. "Yonder,

over the other side of the camp. Hey, Mister Maxwell, what's wrong?"

Back in the direction of the camp, but farther out, someone bawled out a loud curse. It ended very suddenly. Maxwell was already whirling his horse and the men with him who had also guessed what was happening east of the camp, hooked their horses. Those two night-herders were left sitting there with their mouths open.

Evidently the outlaws had come on to the camp, not from the west, but from the southeast. They must have skirted around most of the bedding ground to avoid stirring up the cattle, and had then threaded their way to the horse-herd from below, not above, the camp.

As Grant Maxwell and his three men raced into the camp the cook yelped at them for stirring up dust, and a rider sitting on his bedroll sleepily pulling on his boots, rolled backwards end over end as the horsemen went charging through. At once pandemónium broke loose. No one fired a gun, but Grant Maxwell was half-expecting that to happen as he led the charge out the far side of the camp.

Men were howling back there, angry and completely nonplussed. The cowboy who had been disconsolately trying to pull on his boots jumped up and down in his stockinged feet cursing, wider awake at this moment than he would be again throughout the entire day.

A large, black-headed man, as thick through as a

small fir tree and holding a Winchester in one big fist, stood like stone trying to see where those sudden charging horsemen had gone. He did not speak until someone yelped that it was raiders after the horses, then he bellowed in a roaring voice for every man to grab his gun and race out there.

Grant Maxwell saw the rope corral one moment before it suddenly disintegrated, scattering frightened saddlehorses in all directions. One horse, with a dark saddle stain upon its back, moved out of Maxwell's path, but not very energetically, and that was all he had to see to realize he was too late. The outlaws had already made the switch and were on their way again.

Without slackening speed, Maxwell called to his men. As he did so he yanked loose the lariat kept snug to his saddle-swells and shook out a loop. "Get fresh horses!" he yelled. "Rope fresh animals!"

The cowboys scattered in pursuit of loose stock while the alarmed men from the cow camp raced out—and found only three ridden-down animals with saddle-stains still hovering in the place where the remuda had been.

Grant Maxwell roped a powerful buckskin horse that was running like the wind one moment, and the very next moment, when he felt the soft touch of the rope around his neck, skidded to a sudden halt on all four feet. He was a wise range animal; fighting a lariat only made being caught that much more painful.

Maxwell did not know where the other men were as he stepped down, jerked loose his latigo and yanked up the billet, then, sliding an arm under both saddle and blanket, stepped swiftly up beside the buckskin and re-saddled. Bridling took a little longer, but he was finishing with that when a man on foot suddenly appeared, knelt methodically and aimed his carbine.

"Don't move!" the rangeman snarled at Maxwell. "Step up to that horse's head with both hands away from your body!"

Maxwell saw the kneeling man across the seating leather of his saddle, and called to him. "Henderson? This is Grant Maxwell."

The rifleman did not move. "I said—*step to the head of that horse!*"

Maxwell swore and did as he had been told. Then he faced the kneeling man, arms wide, and tried a second time. "Henderson, I'm Grant Maxwell. My crew and a Pinkerton man have been trailing a band of outlaws since yesterday. The outlaws raided your remuda. We can't catch them without fresh horses. I'll fetch the animals back, Henderson, but we've got to take them, otherwise those damned renegades will get away."

The kneeling man stood up, slowly, and lowered his carbine as he approached Maxwell cautiously. Finally, close enough to make the recognition, he said, "I'll be damned. You *are* Grant Maxwell." He eased the carbine all the way down and Maxwell let his arms fall back to his sides.

"We've been on their trail since yesterday, and all night," he explained again to the thick, black-headed cowman. "They beat us to your remuda."

The cowman said, "How many of them?"

Maxwell repeated the number Jess had mentioned. "Three. But that's only a guess. Originally there were more. One escaped, I shot another one, and there was a wounded feller, but he died over on my side of the mountains. Henderson, if you can catch some horses, shag after us, we may need the help." Maxwell turned and stepped up across the powerful, big buckskin horse. The black-headed cowman watched as Maxwell turned and went racing away into the night. For a moment longer the burly man stood looking, then he whirled and went lumbering back in the direction of his cow-camp, calling for his riders to catch horses, if they could, and get their guns.

Maxwell guessed the outlaws were now riding northward. They would not risk heading west, the direction Maxwell's men had come from, and they dared not ride eastward, in the direction of the town of Laramie. Southward were all those cattle; they would stampede, probably, if a band of fleeing men charged into them, but also they would slow down horsemen who could not afford to be slowed down. That left the northward country, and Maxwell got the 'feel' of the buckskin horse as he headed up in that direction. Once, when he was a long way out, he thought he heard a gunshot back in the direction of the cow camp, and groaned. If someone got killed back there, since the outlaws were already gone, it would have to be either one of his men or one of the men at the cow camp, and that would be a real tragedy.

But that was the only sound, and it was not repeated.

He paused twice, trying to pick up the sound of horsemen either ahead of him or farther back, and the last time he did this, the dawn-lighted morning began turning genuinely dull blue again, which meant the new day was on hand, so he sat there a bit longer than he had done at the earlier halt, scanning the range until he saw three fleeing riders, heading northward, but even as he watched, they veered slightly to the east. Evidently they had also seen Grant Maxwell and elected to change course in order to get a little more country between where they were and where Grant Maxwell was.

He lifted the buckskin into a long-reaching lope, which was not a run, and held him to it. A horse could move like that for a surprising length of time without getting winded.

Someone whooped so far back it sounded like a fading echo. Grant twisted to look back. There were four men coming in his direction at a run. They were spread out over about a mile of soft-lighted rangeland. He thought one of them was Jess Farley, but at that distance, with such poor visibility, he could not be certain. The only sure thing he could rely upon was the fact that those were definitely friends back there; the outlaws were far ahead.

Chapter Eighteen

FORTED-UP!

No one's luck held for ever, and those who oppose the law are enormously out-numbered by those who believe in the law. Those fleeing outlaws had made good still another escape, something at which they were undeniably very experienced, and they had been lucky up until the day one of their band had been wounded down at Fort Collins. After that, as though Al King's blood-atonement were the signal, their luck turned bad. Even though they had fresh horses under them again, they were now able to see in broad daylight, out in open country, the size of the opposition. Not only were there what appeared to be six or seven hard-riding men scattered out behind them in flinging pursuit, but much farther back it looked as though that many more men were coming on from the direction of the cow camp.

Worst of all, perhaps, was the loss of both night-cover and forest-cover. They were out in the open, and although there were more mountains, more forests, on ahead in the northward distance, there was only one way they could hope to reach that protection—if all that furious pursuit could be diverted—and that was very unlikely.

Grant Maxwell was aware of these factors as his powerful borrowed buckskin horse ran belly-down through the chill of dawn. Maxwell was a large man; fortunately, the buckskin was a large horse. Large enough to carry Maxwell as though the burden across his back was half of what it was.

To Maxwell's way of thinking, those fleeing men could turn directly northward, and lose part of the distance between themselves and their angry pursuers, or they could bear off more to the east, and run the risk of meeting riders near Laramie, who would almost certainly join the chase.

The outlaws were like men running down a narrowing funnel.

Looking back, Maxwell could see riders fairly close, as well as far back. They were scattered out across the plain like a small army, and they were coming on with the kind of bleak resolve that meant trouble for the men up ahead.

Maxwell checked his horse a little, to conserve its great power and wind. He could tell simply by watching that the outlaws were allowing their stolen horses to race unchecked, and while desperation might dictate such a course, eventually those animals were going to falter from plain exhaustion.

The outlaws were riding close, as a group. Maxwell saw them slow their checked-up mounts for a moment, as though they were yelling to one another, then one man dropped back and bent low in a twisted way and moments later Maxwell caught sight of paper fluttering in the clear air. The outlaws were jettisoning their loot! At least they were scattering part of it. Maxwell had time to wonder if the men behind him would be diverted by this ruse. According to Jane King, the outlaws had between eighteen and twenty thousand dollars with them. The men riding behind Maxwell were paid anywhere from nine to twelve or fifteen dollars a month. If they saw fifty- and hundred-dollar bills on the ground as they raced along, the temptation would be great, no doubt about it.

Most important, to Maxwell's way of thinking, though, was the desperation up ahead that would make those outlaws try this trick. The outlaws knew they were not going to be able to escape, without a miracle.

The big buckskin horse kept up his powerful rush; at least to him those fluttering greenbacks meant nothing. He had his eyes fixed upon the horsemen up ahead. Maxwell could see that the distance was closing between himself and the renegades. He was still not in carbine range, but he would be shortly. He twisted to look back—and saw a rider do an audacious thing. As the man's horse sped along the cowboy dropped down the side of the animal and, on the run, scooped up one of those greenbacks. Another time Maxwell would have smiled. Now, because that horse back there had been running a long time, was sweaty and had 'shrunk' since being rigged out, Maxwell held his breath, half expecting the cinch to be loose enough for the saddle to turn, and dump the rider.

It didn't happen. Either the cincha was not that loose, or the horse had high enough withers to prevent the rig from turning. As the cowboy came back upright in his saddle Maxwell could see him stuffing something into a shirt pocket. Then, Maxwell smiled.

Up ahead the outlaws had stopped scattering money. They were heading towards something in the middle distance that looked like the upper one-third of a soddy. It was some kind of structure, because there were several corrals behind it, and south of it was a partially-built log barn.

Maxwell hauled his horse back still more. The chase was about to end. North of Maxwell a speeding horse came abreast, then sped onward. This rider was now in the lead. Maxwell saw him lean and jerk out a Winchester as he rode towards the outlaws. The distance was still too great, but that cowboy up there fired anyway, twice.

The outlaws seemed motivated by the sound of gunfire to make a final great effort to reach that soddy up ahead. Maxwell held his horse to an easy lope, which gave the other pursuers an opportunity to catch up. Jess Farley came up nearby and reined over, also holding his borrowed horse down to an easy lope. Jess did not look the least bit excited as he called over, saying, "End of the trail, Boss. If there's anyone at that squatters' place they'll be held hostage."

Jess would have made a good cavalry sergeant; he

may have missed his calling. Maxwell said, "Where's the Pinkerton man?" and Jess shrugged.

"Last I saw, he was back at the cow camp talking thirty mile an hour to a hoppin' mad cowboy who caught him saddlin' one of those fresh horses."

Maxwell had a sudden misgiving. "There was a gunshot back there."

Jess nodded. "That was me convincin' a feller about nineteen years old he didn't really have the drop on me. I didn't hit him. I didn't try to hit him. But he thought I did and threw up his hands." Jess raised an arm. "There they go."

The outlaws had disappeared inside the partially completed log barn. Maxwell waited to see them rush out the opposite end, but they did not do it, which meant they intended to fort up behind those logs. It was a very formidable fortification, too, except for a couple of things: one was called food, the other was called water.

Maxwell kept his horse at a lope. With Jess beside him, with other men converging from as far as a mile northward, it did not take very long for the homesteaders' place to be loosely surrounded.

There was no gunfire. Maxwell's men as well as the rangeriders who worked for the man named Henderson whose camp had been thrown into turmoil an hour earlier, were experienced enough to know the range of a Winchester carbine. They walked their horses the last few hundred yards and afterwards sat out there, eyeing the log barn.

Maxwell made a long study, then looked around as the burly, black-headed cowman rode up, and said, "No one home, Henderson, thank God."

The dark man squinted towards the barn. "That's gratitude for you," he exclaimed. "I lent those squatters the running-gear and teams to haul them damned logs down here." He looked over at Maxwell. "I know what you're thinking. But all squatters aren't the same."

Maxwell denied that implication. "I wasn't thinking any such a thing."

Henderson did not pursue this. Instead, he said, "Well, those outlaws of yours interest me, Grant. Did you see the size of some of those notes they flung out to slow us down? Twenty- and fifty- and even hundred-dollar greenbacks. They sure as hell didn't get that kind of money around Jelm. They must have a regular fortune with 'em."

"Between eighteen and twenty thousand—less what they threw away back there," said Maxwell, enjoying the look of awe on the other cowman's face. "It's a long story. I'll give you the particulars when this is over, if I get a chance. Right now—how do we smoke them out of there?"

Henderson made a soft little clucking sound. "That is an *awful* lot of money."

Maxwell said, "Your cattle are going to scatter," and Henderson, squinting back towards the log barn, agreed, "So they are, for a fact. Well, that can't be helped right now, can it?"

"You don't have to stay," replied Maxwell. "We can keep them bottled up over there. They can't be crazy enough to try rushing out. Otherwise, my boys and I will just sort of get comfortable and wait. When the sun's directly overhead, it must get damned hot inside those four log walls, with no roof."

Henderson said, "I'll send a man on to Laramie. They got enough lawmen over there to make up a small army. . . . By the way, is there a reward of any of those fellers?"

Grant had no idea. "As far as I know, there isn't, but I'm no authority on them. There is a Pinkerton feller riding with us. He's the man wearing the gray suit with the cloth round his head. Maybe he would know." Maxwell looked over. "Why?"

Henderson made an outflung gesture with one arm. "Why? My cattle will be scattered, my men are over there when they should be at the gathering ground— my whole damned routine's been upset and won't get back to normal for another day or two. Now you know that's no way to operate a cow outfit. I figure I'm entitled to some compensation. Is there something wrong with that?"

Maxwell smiled. "No."

Henderson seemed to think his position needed additional defense, because he said, "Sure as hell you aren't going to just write off all the time you and your boys have put in on this, are you? If a man's got to donate his time, I sure can think of a lot better ways to do it than maybe get shot by some low-down outlaws hiding inside a half-walled log barn."

Maxwell agreed again. If Henderson needed reassurance Maxwell was perfectly willing to give it. All Maxwell felt real concern about was taking those men in the homesteaders' roofless log barn. "Send a rider to Laramie for the law, if you want to," he said, and dismounted from the big buckskin horse, hauled out his carbine, stood hip-shot studying the distant log structure. "Any chance of those squatters showing up?" he asked, and Henderson, still in the saddle, could not truthfully say.

"Probably not. When cowmen leave home at dawn it's usually to work the range. When squatters do it I'd say it's so's they can drive a wagon into town, get their supplies, and get back again before dark. If they went to Laramie they sure as hell won't be back until late. Don't worry about them. Like I said, they're not the regular run-of-the-mill homesteaders."

Maxwell looked up. That was the second time Henderson had said that. "What's different about them?"

The mounted man swiftly looked away, pretending to make a menacing study of the forted-up outlaws inside the log barn. "Just different is all," he muttered, and started to change the subject. "Those fellers might be able to stay in there—"

Maxwell leaned on his grounded carbine. "Henderson, what is different about these squatters?"

"Well . . . I'm fixing to marry one of them." Henderson pushed it out so fast the words ran together, then he looked down at Maxwell, his dark face truculent. "They are decent, hard-working people from Iowa. There's this girl . . . this *woman* . . . who came west with the homesteader and his wife."

Maxwell turned back to studying the log barn, and it finally dawned on him why a cowman had gone out of his way to help a squatter haul logs and erect a barn. "It's fine with me," he said to Henderson, without looking up again. "Congratulations. Now, will you send a rider to Laramie?"

Henderson promised to do that. He fell to studying the barn again from the saddle. "They are awful quiet over there."

Maxwell's reply was laconic. "We're out of range."

"You sure you won't need us to hang around?"

Maxwell shook his head. "You've got a gather to work. We can handle it until the law arrives."

Henderson said, "About the horses . . ."

Maxwell finally looked up. "I'll see that they are brought back. And we're right obliged for the loan of them." He smiled slightly. "If there's a charge, tack it on what you figure is due you from the reward."

Henderson lifted his reins to depart. Over inside the log barn someone with a hat atop a carbine barrel tried to draw fire. It was such an obvious ruse no one was interested.

The sun was climbing. It was going to be another hot day.

Chapter Nineteen

MAXWELL'S RUSE

Jess Farley made a circuit of the riders after Henderson had pulled out all but one of his men. That one went streaking in the direction of Laramie. When Jess got over where Grant Maxwell was standing in the shade of the buckskin horse, he dismounted and said, "If they got canteens they'll be able to last out the day. If they don't, they'll have something in mind."

Maxwell soberly nodded. "Like giving each of us a hundred dollars."

Jess tugged at his chin. "That would sure set a man up for a summer of loafing round a mountain lake, fishing and lying around, wouldn't it?"

Maxwell looked at his rangeboss. Farley's dark gaze was ironic. When he saw Maxwell's glance he said, "Nobody'd take it, of course. There's too many of us who wouldn't. . . . Maybe we could chum them out of there."

Maxwell doubted that very much. "Henderson's got them for horse-stealing, the law wants them in Colorado and probably a couple of other places. They aren't going anywhere but straight up or straight down, and they damned well know it. You walk out

170

there making mewing sounds, Jess, and if they don't kill you the moment you step into range, they'll use you for a hostage."

Farley listened, then sighed. "The trouble with successful men, Boss, is that they are always so damned practical," he said, and reached to draw forth his carbine. "It'll take that cowboy more'n an hour to reach Laramie, and it'll probably take another hour for the law down there to shake its stumps and head back here, plus an hour to reach us. That'll put it pretty close to noon."

Maxwell said, "What of it? We've got all the time it'll take. We're not going anywhere and we don't have a gather to work."

"I was just thinkin' that in all that time we'd ought to be able to figure out a way to get those fellers out of there."

Maxwell was perfectly agreeable to that. "How?"

Jess stepped into horse-shade and pondered a long while, looking from beneath his tugged-low hatbrim towards the log barn. "I don't know," he eventually said. "But there's sure got to be a way."

Someone inside the barn tried a long shot. There was no way to tell in which direction he was firing, and neither the man nor his gun was visible. Jess Farley wagged his head, whether at the obvious stalemate, or whether it was in disgust that a man would waste bullets like that, was hard to tell.

Grant Maxwell turned as a rider approached from the rear. It was the Pinkerton detective. He was soiled and rumpled and slouched in the saddle, but as he came up and halted, then stepped down, his expression showed the same hard, unrelenting resolve, only now it was not masked by his customary wraith-like smile.

Maxwell turned back to watching the log barn and let Verrill come over or not, as he chose. As far as Jess was concerned, Verrill could have been standing there all the time; Jess did no more than glance at him, then glance away.

"What we need," said Verrill, "is a Gatling gun."

It was such a preposterous thing to say that Jess answered with an equally as preposterous suggestion. "I'd settle for a bolt of lightning to strike just inside the barn." He turned to get back astride his horse and start the long ride out and around where the other riders were standing or squatting, as the heat increased steadily.

Verrill looked after Farley. "What's eating on him?" he growled, and Maxwell let it go past. He asked how Verrill was feeling, and got a brusque answer.

"For all I've been through, I'm feeling fine. Did you know that one of those damned fools back at the cow camp almost shot me?"

Maxwell let that go past, too. "This is likely to take a long time. You could ride on down to Laramie, if you wanted to, see a doctor for your head and rest up a bit. I doubt that they'll try sneaking out of there until night-fall."

Verrill, who had come this far, had no intention of

dropping out now. "No, thanks," he muttered. "I'll stay."

Maxwell looked at the soddy, which was between the log barn and where he was standing with the detective. It offered no problem, getting that much closer to the log barn. If a man walked crouched over, they could not see him from the barn as long as he kept the upper wall and roof of the soddy between himself and the barn. But getting that much closer did not offer much. Still, Maxwell was tired of just standing out there, so he said, "Watch for someone to poke a gun barrel out," and started away, angling to keep the soddy between himself and the men inside the barn.

Verrill stood between the two horses skeptically watching Maxwell's progress. He seemed not as certain as Maxwell was, but there was no danger.

Maxwell found that this particular soddy had one of those regular doors, the kind that had a sort of earthen entry way on both sides leading down to it. For no particular reason except that he had nothing better to do, Maxwell pushed over the door and stepped inside.

Every soddy had the same moldy, musty smell, even when there were womenfolk to try and keep the place aired out and freshened up with flowers—in season—and toilet water otherwise. Even in the middle of summer when the ground was baked up above, down inside a soddy the smell, and the coolness, remained.

This soddy was not too different from the others Maxwell had seen, except the furniture was better. Somewhere, it had graced a good home. Henderson had said back in Ohio. There were three elegant gilt mirrors, two fine old carved poster-beds, and even the table with its lace-trimmed cloth was entirely out of place in an underground dwelling.

One corner was curtained off. Maxwell did not look over there. One of those elegant mirrors was directly across from the doorway. Maxwell saw himself, and was shocked at the gray stubble, the lines that had been deep-etched over the past twenty-four hours, and the uncompromising expression. The other two mirrors were on the side walls. Maxwell, still in the doorway, had a sudden, daring idea. He considered it a long time, then eventually he went inside, took down all three mirrors and lugged them back out of the soddy and, awkward as they were, and heavy, he crouched low and stalked back where Verrill was waiting.

Jess rode up, having completed his circle, and sat looking dumbly at what his employer had taken from the soddy. Finally, in his most laconic voice, Jess said, "You figuring on shaving?"

Maxwell motioned for Jess to dismount. He handed him one of the mirrors. He handed another one to Norman Verrill. The third one he took himself, and, canting a look at the sun over his shoulder, he maneuvered his mirror until it caught sunlight in a blinding flash of brilliance. He focused the white-hot glare until it shone against the distant opening of the log barn.

Verrill and Farley got the idea and knelt to do the same. It was early enough in the day so that the sun was blindingly hot and fiery, even when a man glanced upwards out of squinted eyes, with his hat-brim pulled down. When that incredible brilliance was concentrated in three mirrors and reflected towards the log barn, it shot a threefold glare across the intervening distance that no one could face.

Maxwell told Jess to get closer, to balance Maxwell's mirror as well as his own, and as soon as Farley was in position the cowman stood up, raised a hand to shield his eyes, and over at the barn someone squawking about the increased heat and the blinding glare made Maxwell smile. He said, "Jess, maybe there *is* a way to get them out of there."

Farley was doubtful. "Them logs won't start burning, if that's what you got in mind." Jess squinted to study the glare, then he said, "It'll increase the heat on 'em, all right, but all they got to do is get up against the near-side wall to avoid most of that."

Maxwell turned and called in another rider by signaling with his upraised arm. As the cowboy loped on over the Pinkerton detective who, unlike Farley, had guessed there was to be more to Maxwell's ruse than just the heat and the blinding shaft of reflected light, watched and kept silent.

When the cowboy came up—it was Chet—Maxwell told him to get down and take Farley's place

175

between the mirrors. Then he said, "If you drop one, or if you let the beam angle off so's they won't be blinded when they try to look over here, you're going to get someone killed. Me, probably. Get into position, Jess; let him have the mirrors and get your carbine." Farley obeyed without a word. When he turned back from yanking forth his saddlegun Grant Maxwell was already moving forward, back in the direction of the soddy. Jess finally understood. He muttered something to himself, and went after Maxwell.

With that blinding light filling the doorway of the partially-completed barn there was no way for the men inside to see anything in that direction. That was what Grant Maxwell was gambling on. Gambling his *life* on, because he did not halt when he reached the soddy, but eased around it and crawled forward. Behind him Jess did the same, but Farley, who was a simple, uncomplicated, direct man, did not believe in tricks like this. He especially did not put store in them when his life was on the line. He cocked the Winchester and held it two-handed, ready for instant use. Then he followed his employer directly into the unbelievably bright glare of that reflection, his face tightened with equal parts of resolution and misgivings.

Maxwell had a particular advantage: he did not have to look back into that blinding brilliance. But he did not believe the men up ahead were fools. They might initially, as Jess had done, think the idea

behind that white-hot light was to increase their discomfort inside the log walls where a pitiless sun was beating downward, but eventually one of them was going to guess the *real* purpose, and that would be the moment when Grant Maxwell would be in his greatest danger.

He hurried to get closer before that moment arrived. Behind him, Jess hurried too, but when he was less than a hundred yards from the doorless wide opening into the barn, Jess halted, knelt, raised his carbine and waited.

Maxwell got closer. He was no more than about two hundred feet away when someone inside the barn fired a carbine. Grant dropped flat. Two carbines opened up, next, but Maxwell saw no nearby eruptions of earth and he did not hear close-whining bullets. He was almost ready to believe those blinded men were firing without being able actually to see him, when someone over there inside the barn cursed in a fierce voice, and when this man fired his six-gun instead of a carbine, Maxwell saw the muzzle blast around the edge of the doorless opening, and heard the slug hit hard into the ground only a yard to his right.

That same fierce-bawling voice was telling the other forted-up men what was happening outside. Grant saw a startled man appear suddenly, straining to look beyond the reflection. Jess fired. That man went backwards in a wild sprawl.

Again the six-gun crept round the log wall and fired

a round. Maxwell heard that bullet strike into the ground too, and he settled with his elbow resting, both hands up, one supporting the other, waiting. When the six-gun came around the next time Grant caught sight of a piece of blue-shirted chest and squeezed off his shot. The other gun exploded skyward, and inside the fort someone let go with a shout, not of pain, evidently, but of shock, or perhaps desperation. A man suddenly appeared up over the front wall, bent low over the neck of a horse.

Maxwell rolled over and called to Jess, but Farley was already waiting when the rider burst out.

It was a foolhardy thing to attempt—unless, of course, as that outlaw probably thought, he had no choice other than to surrender, and that meant a hangrope, so as bad as this last chance was, he did not really have any other. He shot out through the doorway, the horse hit that blinding light, threw up its head in panic and astonishment, and faltered just once. But that was enough. Jess fired, Grant Maxwell fired, and over beside the soddy someone else with a carbine let fly with one round.

The crouching outlaw took those hits hard, just as the horse recovered and lunged ahead in a frightened leap, like a large rabbit, and lit down running westerly, back in the direction of the cow-camp, as hard as he could race.

But the outlaw rode him only a dozen yards, and he was hanging up there loose and lumpy even before he finally got over-balanced and slid down, both feet

clear of the stirrups, and hit the ground so hard he bounced. But he was beyond caring.

Chapter Twenty

WHERE THE TRAIL FORKED

It was over before the men could kick out their horses and run in close enough to lend a hand. Jess lowered his carbine, stood up slowly, and without looking anywhere but directly ahead, he started moving. He seemed to believe there was still one left, inside the barn. Grant Maxwell also went ahead, but he was less anxious. He had not seen the man very well who had been trying to hit him with a six-gun, but he knew he had put a bullet into him. Whether the man was dead or alive, he was no longer capable of fighting, Grant was sure of that as he approached the doorless barn opening, then slid swiftly around it and got inside. There were two men lying inside, both dead. It did not take a coroner's examination to be certain of that. Both had been hit near the breastbone. Neither outlaw had moved after he had landed on the ground.

Jess spoke from beyond the barn, without raising his voice. "Boss . . . ?"

Maxwell answered in the same quiet fashion. "Both finished, Jess. Come on in."

Farley appeared in the doorway. Moments later several riders loped up. Norman Verrill came too, slightly breathless. He had not bothered to mount his horse; he had made the sprint on foot. But he only ducked his head in, saw the dead men, then turned and ran back to the one who had fallen off the running horse.

Chet and the other Maxwell riders pushed on inside. There were two terrified saddled horses crowding in a corner, which the sight of men seemed to calm a bit. The gunfire had undoubtedly frightened the animals into their present state of terror. Despite the roofless condition of the unfinished barn, the inside smelled strongly of burnt powder.

Verrill came rushing back, shouldered through at the doorway and without more than glancing at the corpses, hurried on over and soothingly talked his way up to the horses. He rummaged the first set of saddlebags and came up with nothing, but the second set were filled with money. Verrill removed those bags from behind the cantle, slung them over his shoulder, and somehow this created a noticeable transformation in the man. He smiled at Grant Maxwell, his face lighting up with a variety of pleasantness Maxwell would not have thought Verrill capable of showing.

Maxwell began punching out the spent casings from his gun as he said, "Jess, tie these two across their saddles. Get that other one out there tied over leather, too."

Farley nodded. "His horse run off."

180

"Then tie him behind someone," ordered Maxwell, shoving in fresh loads from his belt, and looked over at the Pinkerton man whose genuine smile was almost as hard for Maxwell to stomach as his false smile. "Tie him behind Mister Pinkerton's saddle. They belong to him now." Grant walked out of the barn.

Chet was standing there. Grant told him to take the three mirrors back and put them in the soddy. "And don't break one," he cautioned. "After you've done that, let's head for Laramie."

The other riders pitched in to help Jess and Chet. Maxwell went over to the well, let the bucket down, cranked it back up, removed his hat, bent far over and doused himself first, then he drank deeply. The sun was getting hotter by the minute.

Verrill came over to also get a drink, still with the bulging saddlebags slung across a thick shoulder. He looked like a pirate, with the bandage round his head slightly askew, his face gaunt, dark, lined and stubbled. His clothing was ruined and instead of having a shellbelt, he had a six-gun shoved into the waistband of his trousers. As he took the bucket when Maxwell offered it, and bent to let it down by the rope, he said, "If there's a reward I'll see that you get it, Mister Maxwell."

Grant watched as the younger man hauled up the bucket of water. He was *Mister* Maxwell again. "What about that cash they scattered over the plain back by the cow camp?" he asked the detective. "Someone'll have to go back for that, but it's not going to be me or my men. We're heading south as soon as we've handed over the bodies to the law in Laramie."

Verrill drank deeply and blew out a big breath afterwards. Then he drank again before putting the bucket aside. "I'll go back for that money, Mister Maxwell. Likely won't get it all, will I?"

Grant said, "Likely you won't. Likely, too, that if Henderson's crew hadn't pitched in, *Mister* Verrill, you wouldn't have got *any* of it. Maybe they're entitled to the few bills they'll try to hold out on you."

Verrill did not disagree. "A man can't condone dishonesty, but I reckon he can figure something; like that's sort of payment, can't he?"

Maxwell said, "Suit yourself," and went back where his horse was. Jess and the other men had the corpses lashed fast. Everyone was mounting up and no one looked particularly pleased even though they had triumphed. Norman Verrill was the last one to get astride as they turned southeastward in the direction of Laramie.

Nothing was said for a couple of miles. Several men slouched along reloading weapons, and others kept an eye on the soggily swaying bodies. Eventually Verrill came up front to ride beside Maxwell. Jess, who had been up there, deciding Verrill and Maxwell had something to discuss, dropped back. He did not especially care about riding with Norman Verrill anyway.

Neither did Grant Maxwell, but he had less choice. The detective stated that he had been going over recent events in his mind on the ride towards town, and although he was dog tired and worn down, he thought he should ride back to the ranch with the Maxwell crew.

It required very little perspicacity for Grant Maxwell to figure that out: Verrill had decided he had better go back and get the girl, otherwise the cowmen might encourage her to slip away. Maxwell said, "Suit yourself. But we're not going to waste much time in Laramie, so if there's a delay about getting rid of these bodies, that'll be your end of it. We'll keep right on heading southward."

They eventually reached the southward road. Jelm lay down it, and if Maxwell and his crew turned off then and there, they still wouldn't reach the ranch until very late that night.

But they did not turn southward because, up ahead about a half-mile, that rider Henderson had sent to Laramie hailed them. He had recognized Maxwell. With him were eleven other riders, every one armed with a carbine slung forward under the saddle-fender. Maxwell rode on across the road heading for the posse.

He expected to meet Craig Myers, the resident deputy at Laramie, and perhaps the Chief of City Police, but although Myers was there, the Chief was not, and the other riders were professional possemen whose names Deputy Myers had on hand because they were good at trailing, and they were also available for immediate service, night or day.

Maxwell knew the deputy and nodded when they came close and halted their horses. Verrill introduced himself. Deputy Myers shook and smiled, and asked about the dead men. It did not take very long to tell that story. Verrill did most of the talking, but as far as Grant Maxwell was concerned, since he told it all reasonably well, there was no need to interrupt.

When the recitation was over, Myers, who was a long, lean, freckled man with a friendly face but a square jaw, said that he would require signed, notarized statements from everyone who had participated in the pursuit and the final, fatal battle. Particularly at the battle.

Maxwell considered asking Myers to ride down to his ranch for that. But in the end he shrugged and let Myers herd him and his crew on into town. He was reluctant every foot of the way. He had no way of knowing riding on into town would provide him with an answer, and a solution, to something that would otherwise have remained a bothersome riddle ever after.

Laramie was a busy town, larger by far than almost any other town in Wyoming, excepting Cheyenne of course. It sat upon the plain, vulnerable to every blast of wind that blew, and during winter when the wind came out of the north, a man could wear everything he owned and the cold would knife right through to chill the marrow in his bones.

It was also a hub for trade and commerce, and with the advent of homesteaders its mercantile establishments were flourishing even more successful than they had back during the Indian wars when Laramie had made its living off the army.

To Grant Maxwell and his riders, Laramie was slightly overwhelming. It made them uncomfortable, but this was not, as people often thought, the result of so much noise and activity; it was the result of being simply more human beings in a place that already had more than enough other human beings. Maxwell's men were accustomed to being individuals. It was that stripping rangemen naked of their individuality that really made them dislike towns.

They took back streets, at Deputy Myers' suggestion, with their cavalcade, and left the corpses off at a doctor's buggy-shed, then went on over to Myers' combination jailhouse and office to give their depositions. Gradually, the Pinkerton man reassumed his normal personality. With the cowmen, he had been tolerated, and that had subdued him, but back in civilization again he became more like he had first appeared to Grant Maxwell. In fact, after Grant gave his statement to Myers, had his signature witnessed and was finished, Verrill asked to see the deposition, to check its accuracy, and because Maxwell's anger was stirring he rose and said he would wait outside at the tie-rack. He left the office, stood in the shade of an old warped wooden awning out front, and watched people go past on the plankwalks, and in rigs and wagons out in the wide, dusty roadway.

A battered stage came down through town from the

north and veered towards a company depot where hostlers rushed out to change the hitch and grease wheels, while two men wearing green eyeshades and sleeve garters pitched luggage up top to the driver's helper who lashed things down atop the coach.

Then Maxwell saw her, and froze where he stood. She was wearing a bonnet and a clean dress, but her tanned arms and throat and her piquant face were unmistakable. He may have projected something, perhaps his surprise, because she turned—and saw him standing down there out front of the sheriff's office. She, too, stood a long while without moving.

Maxwell untracked and started across the road and northward. He walked slowly and thoughtfully. She came down a short distance to meet him, and when they were facing each other she said, "I had to, Mister Maxwell. I—left a letter for you at the ranch, and up there where your wife is buried I put some wild flowers on her grave, and a little ways off where I'd like for Al to be buried." She made a little fluttery gesture. "If you want, I'll go back to the sheriff's office."

He smiled at her. "No. You can't go back, Jane, even when you want to. Where are you going?"

"San Francisco. I knew some people who moved out there some years back. I—don't know where else to go."

He reached in his pocket and pulled out a flat, worn packet of greenbacks and put them in her hand. "Don't say anything, just take it. Money's no good to people if they don't spend it. Me, I carry the damned stuff around month after month in my pocket, and . . ." He shrugged. "We'll take care of your husband. Maybe, someday, you'll want to come back for a visit. Well, let things die down for a couple of years." He glanced over where someone had just emerged from the deputy's office. It was Jess, and he did not look across the road; he got busy rolling a smoke. When Maxwell looked back he said, "When does your coach leave?"

Jane, who had also seen and recognized Jess, answered quietly. "In a few minutes. As soon as they've finished loading and putting on the new hitch. . . . Mister Maxwell?"

He looked down, knowing what she was going to say. "Yes?"

"I'm very grateful."

He smiled at her. "Promise me one thing: the next time, if he goes bad, don't be so loyal."

Her gray eyes were moist as she said, "There won't be a next time."

Behind them people were boarding the coach, hostlers were standing at the head of the fresh hitch, and the whip was gathering his lines. Grant said, "Goodbye, Jane. One more thing: if you need help, write me. Promise me that?"

She suddenly stood up as tall as she could, kissed him, left salt tears upon his cheek and turned to run back and board the stage. Maxwell walked back across the road where Jess was leaning, smoking. As he came up his rangeboss said, "She got enough money to get where she's going?" and Maxwell smiled. Jess was a hawk-eyed individual.

"She has now. What's Verrill doing in there?"

"Acting like Mister Pinkerton," Farley replied, and blew smoke as the stage swung clear and headed southward down the roadway. He and Grant watched for the tanned, sweet face, waved when they saw her go past, then Maxwell said, "She's young. In a different place she'll try again. I hope to hell she picks a better one next time."

Jess, watching the coach raise dust, made a comment without looking around. "You know what you've got out of all this? A new grave in the cemetery." He turned and regarded his employer. "If she never comes back, it'll be for the best. That means you've got another grave to tend—and you've paid a pretty high price for it."

Maxwell did not think so. "I forgot to ask her about her big sorrel horses," he said. "I think she'd approve. I'm going to give them to those squatters. That little boy of theirs needs something to cotton to." Maxwell looked up as the door opened and his men trooped out.

Jess also looked around, and he said, "You fellers know how much riding we got to do when we get back home and go to work for a change? Let's get moving!"

Grant Maxwell looked southward. The coach was no longer in sight, but its dust hung in the still, hot daylight like a dun banner. Then he turned without another word and went out to the tie-rack. Verrill came out, then, and hurried to join the mounted men.

Maxwell smiled at him. By the time Verrill got back to the ranch, that stagecoach would be almost a full day on its way.

LAURAN PAINE, under his own name and various pseudonyms, wrote hundreds of novels. His apprenticeship as a Western writer came about through the years he spent in the livestock trade, rodeos and even motion pictures, where he often worked as an extra.

Center Point Publishing
600 Brooks Road • PO Box 1
Thorndike ME 04986-0001 USA

(207) 568-3717

US & Canada:
1 800 929-9108